Lasting Scars

Ballad of Innocence

To my wife and family, whose unwavering love and steadfast presence have been my refuge through every trial and tribulation—this work is devoted with deepest gratitude and enduring love.

A man possesses nothing of true worth until he awakens to the reality that he is summoned to transcendence—called to higher things by a divine purpose that gives meaning to his very existence.

Table of Contents

Prologue

Chlorine Reflections

The chlorine stung Mariana's eyes as she surfaced, lungs burning from holding her breath the full length of the pool. She had pushed herself harder than usual today, feeling the water part seamlessly around her body as she glided beneath the surface. Coach Riley's stopwatch clicked with a satisfying finality.

"Personal best, Garcia! Keep that up and Regionals are in the bag."

Mariana nodded, too winded to speak. She gripped the edge of the pool, taking a moment to collect herself. Her muscles trembled from exertion, a pleasant fatigue that told her she'd given everything. As she pulled herself from the pool, water cascading from her shoulders in silver rivulets, she felt it—that peculiar sensation of being watched, like a phantom touch against her skin.

Across the natatorium, through the foggy glass of the viewing area, stood a boy she vaguely recognized from her English class. Tall, with shaggy dirty blond hair that needed cutting. Richard Vance—Richey, as he insisted everyone call him. He was holding a stack of books—probably waiting for someone—but his eyes were fixed on the pool. On her.

Their gazes connected for just a moment before he looked away, embarrassed at being caught staring. Mariana felt a curious flutter in her chest that had nothing to do with exertion. She'd noticed him before, of course—he sat two rows behind her in English, rarely speaking unless called upon. There was something in his quiet intensity that had always intrigued her, though they'd never exchanged more than a handful of words.

"Garcia! Two-minute break, then I want another lap!" Coach Riley's voice snapped her attention back, the brief connection broken by the sharp command.

Mariana pushed her swim cap back, adjusting the silicone edge where it dug into her forehead. She'd been swimming competitively since she was nine, and at sixteen, the routine was as familiar as breathing. Wake up at 5 AM. Morning practice. School. Afternoon practice. Homework until her eyes burned. Sleep. Repeat. Her life measured in laps and times, each tenth of a second shaved off a personal record a victory to be celebrated.

When she looked up again, searching almost instinctively for that lanky figure behind the glass, the boy was gone. She felt an unexpected pang of disappointment, quickly brushed aside as she reached for her water bottle.

"You're killing it today, Captain," Stephanie said, sliding into the water beside her. "That butterfly was insane. I swear you barely made a splash."

Mariana smiled, pleased by the compliment despite herself. "Thanks. I've been working on my entry. Coach says I'm still lifting my head too much on the turns, though."

"Coach would find something to criticize if you swam like Katie Ledecky," Stephanie rolled her eyes, splashing water playfully. "You worried about Regionals?"

The question hung between them, heavier than it should have been. Regionals meant college scouts. College scouts meant potential scholarships. And scholarships meant everything to Mariana's family.

"Not worried," she said with forced casualness. "Just focused."

Stephanie nodded, understanding the weight behind those simple words. They all knew what was at stake for Mariana—the team captain, the straight-A student, the immigrant daughter carrying her parents' dreams on her shoulders.

"You coming to Jackie's thing on Friday?" Stephanie asked, changing the subject as they both watched Coach Riley scribbling notes on his clipboard, his perpetual frown deepening as he calculated split times.

"Can't," Mariana replied automatically. "Regionals prep. And my birthday dinner with family."

The lie came easily, practiced. It wasn't entirely untrue—her birthday was on Thursday, and her mother would insist on a special dinner. But the real reason was simpler: parties meant questions from her parents, negotiations, implicit disappointment. It was easier to just not ask.

"You should come," Stephanie pressed. "Jackie says her parents are going to be there, so even your mom can't object. And it's your birthday week. Live a little, Captain Perfect."

Mariana winced at the nickname, though she knew Stephanie meant no harm. Captain Perfect. It was meant affectionately, but sometimes felt like a straightjacket—expectations wrapped around her so tightly she could barely breathe.

"I'll think about it," she conceded, knowing she wouldn't.

"Garcia!" Coach Riley's voice boomed across the natatorium. "Break's over. I want to see that 200 fly again, and this time watch those turns!"

Mariana pushed away from the wall, sliding her goggles back into place. As she prepared to dive, a movement in the viewing area caught her eye—a flash of dirty blond hair, a quick turn. But when she looked again, there was nothing.

She shook her head, clearing away distractions. The water called to her, still and blue and waiting. With a deep breath, she dove, feeling the familiar embrace as the pool swallowed her whole.

———

The locker room was a cacophony of slamming metal doors, excited chatter, and the persistent hiss of shower spray. Mariana changed methodically, toweling her hair and slipping into her school clothes with practiced efficiency.

"I'm telling you, Ryan was totally checking you out during that last set," Kayla insisted, applying lip gloss while peering into a small magnetic mirror stuck to her locker door.

"Ryan checks out anything in a swimsuit," Stephanie countered, rolling her eyes. "Besides, Captain's got an admirer of her own."

Mariana looked up sharply from lacing her sneakers. "What?"

"Don't play dumb," Stephanie grinned, nudging her with an elbow. "That quiet guy from English. The one with the hair. He watches you swim at least once a week."

"Richey," Mariana said before she could stop herself.

"Ooh, she knows his name," Kayla teased, joining their conversation with predatory interest. "Spill, Captain. What's the story?"

"There's no story," Mariana said, feeling heat rise to her cheeks. "He sits behind me in English. That's it."

"He's on the football team, right?" Stephanie asked, scrunching her still-damp hair with a towel. "Second-string quarterback or something?"

"Backup to Jimmy," Kayla confirmed. "Kind of cute in that broody way. Not really our circle, though."

Mariana said nothing, zipping her backpack with more force than necessary. There was something uncomfortable about the way they dismissed him, categorizing him so neatly. Not our circle. As if the entire school population could be sorted and labeled like specimens in a lab.

"Anyway," Stephanie continued, oblivious to Mariana's discomfort, "I'm just saying, he looks at you like you hung the moon. You could do worse."

"I don't have time to 'do' anyone," Mariana replied, slinging her bag over her shoulder. "I've got to stop by the library before Bio."

The truth was, she'd noticed Richey long before today. His quiet presence in English class was somehow both unobtrusive and impossible to ignore. He rarely joined the boisterous pre-class conversations, seemed uninterested in the social hierarchy that dominated their high school existence, and had a way of answering questions that revealed he'd thought deeper about the material than most of their classmates.

Once, last semester, when they were reading "The Great Gatsby," he'd made a comment about Gatsby's delusion—that you couldn't recreate the past no matter how desperately you tried—and there had been something in his voice, a kind of raw understanding, that had made Mariana turn in her seat to look at him directly. For a brief moment, their eyes had met, and she'd felt that same flutter she'd experienced at the pool.

Then Mrs. Kowalowski had called on someone else, and the moment dissolved like sugar in water.

She'd learned bits and pieces about him since then, mostly through the osmosis of high school gossip. His parents were divorced. He lived with his dad, who had some kind of drinking problem. He was smart—honors classes across the board—but not social. Some of the football players called him "Richey Broke" because of his thrift store clothes and the ancient flip phone he carried instead of the latest iPhone.

But there was something about him that didn't fit neatly into the box of "poor kid with problems" that others tried to place him in. A dignity, maybe. A quiet determination that Mariana recognized because she carried something similar within herself.

It reminded her of her father in a way. Last month, when she'd been struggling with her AP Chemistry project, staying up until 2 AM with frustration-induced tears, Ricardo had appeared in her doorway. Instead of his usual lecture about responsibility and time management, he'd simply sat beside her at the desk. 'Show me,' he'd said.

Though he hadn't understood the chemistry, he stayed, making her explain each step, his presence alone somehow making the problem clearer. 'You are more than one test, mija,' he'd told her before leaving. 'Remember that.' It was a rare moment of gentleness from her usually stern father, a glimpse of the man beneath the hardworking immigrant whose focus on their future sometimes masked his deep love.

"Earth to Mariana," Stephanie waved a hand in front of her face. "You still with us, Captain?"

Mariana blinked, realizing she'd been lost in thought. The chlorine-scented air of the natatorium surrounded them as they gathered their gear after practice, but her mind had been elsewhere.

"Sorry," she said, tucking her damp hair behind her ear. "Just thinking about tomorrow's meet."

"Sure you were," Stephanie smirked, zipping up her swim bag. "Your mind was definitely not on a certain second-string quarterback."

Mariana felt heat rise to her cheeks. "We should hurry," she said, changing the subject. "Coach Riley wants to lock up, and I promised my mom I wouldn't be late."

The school library was quiet at this hour, most students still in the cafeteria finishing lunch. Mariana claimed her favorite spot near the windows, spreading out her notebooks to review for the afternoon's Geography quiz. The sunlight created dappled patterns across the pages, warming her still-damp hair.

She loved these stolen moments of solitude. The quiet of the library reminded her of being underwater—the world muffled and distant, allowing her thoughts to clarify and settle.

Her parents had high expectations, but they were nothing compared to the standards Mariana set for herself. Perfect GPA. Captain of the swim team. College scholarship. These weren't just goals; they were necessities, foundations for the future she was determined to build. A future worthy of her parents' sacrifices.

Both had left everything behind in Guatemala—family, language, the familiar comfort of home—to give their daughters opportunities they'd never had. Her father worked construction, his hands perpetually rough from labor. Her mother cleaned houses, her back often aching after long days scrubbing floors and bathtubs. They had built a life from nothing, and Mariana would not waste their efforts.

But sometimes, in quiet moments like this, she allowed herself to wonder about the things she might be missing. The ordinary teenage experiences that seemed so insignificant but somehow added up to something important. Parties. Friends. Maybe even a boy who looked at her like she was more than just a collection of achievements.

The sound of books being placed on the table across from her pulled Mariana from her thoughts. She looked up, startled to find herself staring directly at Richey Vance.

He seemed equally surprised, as if he hadn't noticed her until that moment. "Sorry," he said quietly, already gathering his books to leave. "I didn't realize—"

"It's fine," Mariana said quickly. "Plenty of room."

He hesitated, shifting his weight from one foot to the other, then slowly sat, placing his battered copy of "The Grapes of Wrath" between them like a barrier.

They existed in awkward silence for several minutes, each pretending to read while acutely aware of the other's presence. Mariana found herself stealing glances at him—the way his hair fell across his forehead, the serious set of his jaw, the careful way he turned each page as if the book might fall apart in his hands.

"You're really good," he said suddenly, his voice so soft she almost missed it.

She looked up, confused. "What?"

"Swimming," he clarified, color rising to his cheeks. "You're really good. I mean, I don't know much about it, but even I can tell."

Mariana felt that flutter again, ridiculous and unexpected. "Thanks. I've been doing it a while."

"Since you were a kid?"

She nodded. "Nine. My mom thought it was important we learn to swim after a cousin almost drowned back in Guatemala."

It was the most personal thing she'd ever shared with him, and the realization surprised her. Something about his direct blue gaze made it easy to speak honestly.

"Do you like it?" he asked, and the question caught her off guard. Most people assumed she did, or didn't think to ask at all.

"I—" she started, then paused, considering. "Most of the time. Sometimes it feels like... I don't know. Like it's not just swimming anymore. It's everything. My future. My parents' pride. College." She stopped abruptly, embarrassed by her sudden candor. "Sorry. That was a lot."

But Richey was nodding, understanding in his eyes. "I get that. Football's kind of the same way for me. Except it's not even my dream, really. Just a potential ticket out."

"Out of what?" The question slipped out before she could stop it.

Something closed in his expression, a shutter falling. "Just... out. College. Something better."

The bell rang, signaling the end of lunch period, and the moment fractured. They both stood, gathering their books with sudden urgency.

"I should get to class," Mariana said, though Bio was only two doors down.

Richey nodded, already backing away. "Yeah, me too. Sorry again for interrupting your studying."

"You didn't," she said quickly. "It was... nice. Talking."

A small smile touched his lips, transforming his serious face into something gentler. "Yeah. It was."

Then he was gone, disappearing into the stream of students flooding the halls. Mariana stood still for a moment, an unexpected warmth spreading through her chest.

She was going to be late for Bio for the first time in her academic career. And somehow, she couldn't bring herself to care.

———

That evening, Mariana sat at her desk, textbooks spread before her, but her mind kept drifting back to that brief conversation in the library. There had been something in the way Richey spoke about football—not with the typical athletic bravado, but as a means to an end. A practical solution to a problem he didn't name.

Her phone buzzed with a text from Stephanie: *Talked to Jackie. Her parents OK with you sleeping over Friday. NO EXCUSES, CAPTAIN.*

Mariana sighed, knowing she should just decline now. Her mother would probably say no anyway. Sleepovers were rare, strictly regulated events in the Garcia household. But some small, rebellious part of her wanted to go. To step outside the careful boundaries of her life, just for one night.

A soft knock at her door interrupted her thoughts. Her sister Vanessa poked her head in, dark hair falling in a sleek bob around her face.

"Mom says dinner in ten," she announced, then hesitated, a sly smile spreading across her face. "So... I hear Richey Vance was watching you at practice today."

Mariana groaned. "Is nothing private in this school?"

"Nope," Vanessa replied cheerfully, flopping onto Mariana's bed uninvited. "Especially not when it involves Captain Perfect and the mysterious backup quarterback."

"Don't call me that," Mariana said automatically, turning to face her sister. "And he's not mysterious. Just quiet."

"Mmhmm." Vanessa's grin widened. "You know, he helped me once. Last year, when I dropped all my books in the hallway. Most people just walked by, but he stopped and picked everything up. Didn't say much, but he was nice."

Mariana felt an irrational surge of pleasure at this information. "He seems... different. From most of the guys at school."

"Because he doesn't have his head permanently lodged up his own—"

"Vanessa!" Mariana cut her off, fighting a smile.

"Well, it's true." Vanessa shrugged, picking at a loose thread on Mariana's comforter. "Anyway, I approve. If you're looking for that sort of thing."

"I'm not looking for anything," Mariana insisted, but the protest sounded weak even to her own ears. "I'm focused on swimming. And school."

"Right, because those are mutually exclusive with having an actual life." Vanessa rolled her eyes, the wisdom of her fourteen years delivered with absolute conviction. "You know, you're allowed to want things just because you want them. Not because they look good on a college application."

Before Mariana could respond, their mother's voice called up the stairs. "Girls! Dinner!"

Vanessa bounced off the bed, heading for the door, then paused. "You should talk to him. For real, I mean. What's the worst that could happen?"

As her sister disappeared down the hallway, Mariana turned back to her desk, her reflection staring back at her from the darkened computer screen. What was the worst that could happen? She could get distracted. Lose focus. Let her times slip. Disappoint her parents. Miss her shot at a scholarship.

Or maybe, something whispered from a quiet corner of her mind, the worst that could happen is that you'd find out there's more to life than what you've planned for.

She shook her head, pushing away from the desk. Dinner first. Decisions later. One step at a time, just like Coach Riley always said. Just like she'd been doing her whole life.

But as she headed downstairs, Mariana found herself wondering what Richey Vance might be doing right now. If he ever thought about her outside of school. If he'd be at Jackie's party on Friday night.

And for the first time in a long time, she allowed herself to hope for something that had nothing to do with swimming or grades or college.

Just a moment. A conversation. A connection that felt as natural as diving into the deep end of the pool.

Out of League

Richey clutched his books tighter, hurrying away from the pool area, his face burning. She'd seen him watching. Great.

It wasn't the first time he'd wandered past the natatorium during Mariana Garcia's swim practice. Over the past few months, he'd developed a habit of taking the long route to his locker—the one that just happened to pass the glass-walled pool where she trained. He'd tell himself it was merely curiosity, a momentary distraction on the way to somewhere more important. But deep down, he knew better.

There was something about the way she moved through water—graceful, powerful, completely in her element. Something he couldn't put into words but couldn't stop watching either. Like poetry in motion, if poetry were made of chlorine and determination.

But this time, their eyes had met through the foggy glass, and she'd caught him staring. He'd looked away immediately, of course, but not fast enough. The damage was done.

"Dude, where were you?" Daniel fell into step beside him, his perpetually untied shoelaces slapping against the linoleum hallway. "I thought you were grabbing your history book and meeting me by the cafeteria."

Daniel—his best friend since fourth grade, the guy who'd shared his lunch when Richey forgot his, the only person who knew what home was really like. Daniel with his easy smile and his ability to talk to anyone. Daniel who never seemed to doubt himself the way Richey did.

"Got distracted," Richey muttered, adjusting the weight of his backpack, its worn strap digging into his shoulder. The backpack had been new three years ago, a rare splurge from his father during a period of sobriety that hadn't lasted. Now it was fraying at the seams, much like everything else in his life.

"By the swim team?" Daniel wiggled his eyebrows, a knowing smile spreading across his face. "Or one swimmer in particular?"

The fluorescent lights buzzed overhead, casting everyone in the hallway in the same unflattering glow. Richey tried to keep his expression neutral, though he could feel warmth creeping up his neck.

"Shut up. I just got lost in thought." He shoved Daniel lightly, the familiar rhythm of their banter a welcome distraction from the embarrassment still burning in his chest.

"About Mariana Garcia's butterfly stroke, maybe?" Daniel pressed, his voice lowered just enough to avoid being overheard by the streams of students moving around them.

Mariana Garcia. Even her name sounded like it belonged somewhere better than Memorial High—somewhere with proper funding and working water fountains and teachers who didn't look perpetually exhausted. Somewhere Richey didn't belong.

"I don't even know her," he said, which wasn't exactly a lie. He knew her name, knew she sat ahead in English, knew she won medals for the school. Knew that her handwriting was neat and small, that she chewed her pen cap when she was thinking hard, that she always had color-coded notes with highlighted sections. But they'd never spoken. Not really. Just the occasional "excuse me" when passing in the hallway or the silent acknowledgment when he held the door open for her after class.

"Yeah, well, she's out of your league anyway," Daniel said, not unkindly. "Miss Perfect Student, swim team captain. Word is she's never even been to a party."

The words stung more than they should have. Out of your league. A truth Richey had acknowledged to himself many times but somehow more painful when spoken aloud. It wasn't just about social hierarchies or popularity—though God knew Memorial High had enough of those invisible boundaries. It was about trajectories. Mariana was clearly going somewhere. She had purpose, drive, a family who showed up to her meets with homemade signs. She was the kind of student colleges fought over.

And Richey? He was just trying to stay afloat.

"I said I don't know her," he repeated, more firmly this time, as if saying it with enough conviction might make it less pathetic that he'd spent so many afternoons watching her from behind fogged glass.

But as they pushed through the double doors into the main hallway, he couldn't help glancing back toward the natatorium, wondering what it would be like to actually talk to a girl like that—someone with purpose, with passion, with a future as bright as chlorinated water in sunlight.

"Come on," Daniel said, slinging an arm around Richey's shoulders. "Jimmy bailed on the calculus study group, and Mrs. Peterson said we can use her room during lunch. I need to pass this test on Friday or my dad's going to lose it."

Richey nodded, grateful for the subject change. "Yeah, let's go."

As they headed toward the math wing, Richey tried to push thoughts of Mariana from his mind. He had more immediate concerns—like the calculus test, and football practice later, and whether his dad would be sober when he got home.

But the image lingered—Mariana surfacing from the water, droplets cascading from her shoulders, noticing him watching. And for just a moment, before embarrassment had sent him hurrying away, he thought he'd seen something in her expression. Not annoyance or disgust, but... curiosity?

Probably just his imagination. Girls like Mariana Garcia didn't notice guys like him. Not really.

The locker room smelled like it always did—a pungent mix of sweat, deodorant, and the industrial disinfectant the janitors used after practice. Richey changed quickly, pulling his practice jersey over his head and reaching for his cleats.

"Hey, Richey Broke," came a voice from behind, the nickname landing like a stone. "You planning to actually throw a decent pass today, or should we just prepare for Jimmy to save our asses again?"

Chad. Of course it was Chad. Six-foot-three, two hundred and fifteen pounds of lineman muscle and inherited privilege. His father had played college ball for Texas A&M, a fact he mentioned approximately once every seven minutes.

"Leave it, Chad," Richey said, not turning around. He'd learned early that engaging only made it worse.

"Just saying." Chad's voice carried across the locker room, drawing attention they didn't need. "Some of us are trying to get scouted this year. Hard to showcase your blocking when your second-string quarterback can't hit a receiver to save his life."

The words cut deeper than they should have. Richey knew he wasn't a bad quarterback—Coach Kenneck wouldn't have kept him on second string if he was. But he also knew he wasn't Jimmy Prescott, with his cannon arm and family connections and private quarterback coach.

"You do your job, Chad," Richey said evenly, lacing his cleats with practiced precision. "I'll do mine."

He could feel Daniel watching from a few lockers down, ready to jump in if needed. But Richey gave a slight shake of his head. He didn't need saving. Not from this, at least.

Chad snorted. "Sure thing, Broke. Just don't fuck up my highlight reel."

As Chad sauntered away, Richey took a deep breath, controlling the anger that threatened to rise. He was used to the nickname—Richey Broke, a play on his last name and the obvious fact that he didn't have

"You're late," his father said, though Richey knew he wasn't. Practice had ended at five-thirty. He'd been home by five-fifty.

"Sorry," he said anyway, knowing it was easier than arguing. "Practice ran long."

His father snorted. "Football. Waste of damn time if you ask me."

Richey didn't respond. This was an old conversation, one they'd had so many times it had worn a groove in their relationship. His father saw football as a distraction from the immediate—from work, from helping around the house, from the practical realities of their lives. Richey saw it as his only real shot at something better—a scholarship, maybe, or at least connections to a world beyond this small, stained existence.

"I'm gonna shower," he said, already moving toward the hallway, toward the sanctuary of his room with its lock that mostly worked.

"Coach called," his father said, the words stopping Richey in his tracks.

Richey turned slowly. "What?"

"Your coach. Called here earlier." His father took another swig from the bottle. "Something about you practicing with the first team. Said I should be proud."

For a moment—just a moment—Richey felt a flicker of hope. That his father might actually say it. Might actually be proud.

Instead, James Vance laughed, a sound empty of humor. "Told him he was barking up the wrong tree. Football never put food on anyone's table."

The hope withered as quickly as it had bloomed. "Right," Richey said, his voice flat. "Because working at the machine shop has been such a great career move for you."

He regretted the words as soon as they left his mouth. Saw the flash of anger in his father's eyes, the tightening of his jaw.

"What did you just say to me, boy?"

Richey stood his ground, too tired, too disappointed to back down this time. "You heard me."

For a tense moment, he thought his father might get up, might cross the space between them, might do what he'd done too many times before when the bottle was his primary companion. But instead, James Vance seemed to deflate, sinking deeper into his recliner.

"Get out of my sight," he muttered, turning back to the television. "Ungrateful little shit."

Richey didn't need to be told twice. He retreated to his room, the small space that was his alone. Clean, organized, the opposite of the chaos that ruled the rest of the house. A twin bed with a navy comforter, a desk he'd built himself from scavenged wood, a bookshelf filled with library books and a few treasured paperbacks bought with money saved from odd jobs.

He collapsed onto the bed, staring at the ceiling, the adrenaline of confrontation slowly fading from his system. His phone buzzed in his pocket—a text from Daniel.

"Still coming over to study calc tomorrow?"

Richey typed a quick "yeah," grateful for the reminder of something normal, something constant.

His gaze drifted to the small bulletin board above his desk, where he'd tacked a few things—his acceptance letter to the National Honor Society, a ticket stub from the one professional football game he'd ever attended, a photograph of him and his mother from years ago, both smiling.

And, hidden partly behind the NHS letter, a clipping from the school newspaper. A photo of Mariana Garcia accepting a medal at last year's regional swim meet, her smile radiant, water droplets still clinging to her shoulders. He'd cut it out on impulse and had immediately felt ridiculous, like some kind of stalker. But he hadn't thrown it away either.

Out of your league. The words echoed in his mind, a truth he couldn't escape. Girls like Mariana Garcia didn't end up with guys like him. Girls with bright futures and supportive families didn't choose boys with alcoholic fathers and secondhand clothes.

But still. That moment today, when their eyes had met through the glass of the natatorium. The flash of recognition, of acknowledgment.

It wasn't much. Barely anything at all. But in a life with precious few bright spots, Richey found himself holding onto it anyway—this small, improbable connection, this moment when Mariana Garcia, of all people, had seen him.

Not Richey Broke. Not second-string quarterback. Not the boy with the drunk father and the absent mother.

Just him. Just Richey.

It was probably nothing. But as he lay there, surrounded by the evidence of his careful, methodical attempts to build something better than what he'd been given, he allowed himself to wonder.

What if it wasn't?

Friday

Morning Routine

Mariana opened her eyes slowly. A lingering grogginess dulled her senses as the morning light seeped through the window. It was her third alarm. The chirping of birds outside, that familiar, hopeful song, filled the air, always sounding like a promise of a better day. As her vision cleared, the window took shape, and so did the piles of laundry scattered across the room—an unusual sight in her normally tidy space. The chaos was the result of last night's desperate search for her lucky swimsuit.

Maybe Mom will do it later, she thought, rolling her eyes.

Then it hit her — the Regional Swim Meet. She bolted upright, adrenaline cutting through the haze. Mariana paused, pressing a hand lightly against her chest. She felt the familiar flutter—a tight, squeezing sensation that occasionally crept up when the pressure mounted. Her mother called it nerves, but Mariana knew it was more. Breathing carefully, she counted slowly, just like Coach Riley had taught her during one of her first episodes. She'd learned early to hide these moments, especially from Vanessa, who already watched her too closely.

This wasn't just another meet. She was the team captain. Coach Riley had placed his trust in her. The school was counting on her.

She glanced at her phone to check the time. Friday's schedule was going to be tight. Most regional meets happened on weekends, but this year's had been split across Friday and Saturday due to the number of schools participating. Individual events today, team relays tomorrow. Coach Riley had been drilling them about the unusual format for weeks, making sure they understood the importance of pacing themselves across the two days.

Mariana's events were all scheduled for today, which meant missing the last period to get ready. Her 200 freestyle and 100 butterfly were the cornerstones of her college recruitment portfolio. Tomorrow, she'd return to anchor the relay teams, but today was about her individual qualification times.

She wanted to win. She needed to make her team — and her family — proud.

"Breakfast is ready!" her mom's voice called from downstairs.

It had been a long week. Mariana rifled through the mess until she settled on a cute top her sister Vanessa had gifted her yesterday for her birthday. She brushed her hair back into a tight ponytail, smoothing the wisps at her temples with a dab of gel — the same stubborn hairs that always refused to cooperate.

"Your alarm's been going off for fifteen minutes, Mariana," came her mother's voice again.

"I know, Mom. I don't get why I can't hear it the first time," Mariana replied as she adjusted her collar.

"You should try setting it louder," her mom called back.

Vanessa came bounding down the stairs. "No, Mom, please don't — I already have to put up with her twenty-minute alarm as it is!"

"Don't run in the house. Eat your breakfast — we're leaving in ten," their mom called, a final note of authority in her voice.

The sisters finished their breakfast quickly. Their mother took school seriously. A tardy meant trouble — always had. They rushed upstairs, brushed their teeth, double-checked their hair and outfits, then ran back down toward the car.

"Shotgun!" Vanessa shouted, racing to the front seat.

They were close in complexion but opposites in every other way.

Vanessa, the younger of the two, was fiery and bold — always quick with an opinion, even before anyone asked. She lived for the moment, thrived in social scenes, and was rapidly climbing the ladder of popularity at Memorial High. As a sophomore, though, she was still mostly known as *Mariana's* sister — a fact that drove her up the wall. She wore her dark hair in a blunt bob just below the earlobes, hating the fuss of brushing and tying it every morning. She was a little stockier than Mariana, but she had her own spark.

Mariana was taller and leaner, years of swimming shaping her into an elegant silhouette. She was quiet, composed, and deliberate with her words. Swimming gave her peace — the stillness underwater, the sound of nothing but her breath. Her hair, a streaked blend of amber and brown, bore the soft bleach of chlorine and summer sun. Her skin glowed with a golden brown from countless meets held under open skies. And when she smiled, people noticed.

"Mariana, what time is your competition?" their mother asked from the driver's seat.

"Mariana didn't answer at first. Her mind was swimming — literally — with thoughts of strokes, flips, breathing cycles, and everything Coach Riley had drilled into her for years.

'Mariana, I'm talking to you,' her mom repeated, louder this time.

Mariana snapped out of it. 'Six o'clock, Mom. Is Dad going to be there?' She glanced briefly at her mother's hands gripping the steering wheel, noticing the faint lines—lines carved by years of long shifts and sacrifices Mariana couldn't fully grasp.

Her parents had built a life from scratch, leaving behind everything familiar in Guatemala. The weight of that decision was like an invisible current beneath every conversation, every meet, every grade she earned. Her victories felt less like achievements and more like repayments on a debt she never chose but couldn't ignore.

"I don't know, sweetie. You know he's working. He had a delivery all the way to Ohio. He said he'd try."

Her father had only made it to one meet the whole year. She tried not to take it personally, but today mattered.

Her thoughts shifted again — to the meet, then the quiz in geography, and then to Jackie's party.

"Oh — Mom, remember it's Jackie's party tonight. I'm catching a ride with her and sleeping over."

"Yes, sweetie, I remember. Just make sure you call me before bed. I still want to talk to Jackie's mom."

"Sure, Mom," Mariana said, already thinking ahead.

She was looking forward to it. Her birthday had been on Thursday, but she hadn't been able to celebrate with friends. Tonight would be different.

As they neared school, the beige block buildings of Memorial High came into view. It looked tired — rundown. Renovations had begun last year, but at the current pace, Mariana would be long gone before anything finished. The loop in front — the informal drop-off circle — was already filling up. Her friends would be waiting at the steps, trading gossip and stories. She liked listening, even if she rarely joined in.

"Bye, Mom. Love you!" both girls said as they hopped out.

"Have a great day!"

Mariana and Vanessa walked side by side toward the entrance. Their mother watched from the car as her daughters disappeared into the crowd. She smiled, her heart tugging gently. So much had happened to get them here.

She thought of the life they'd left behind. Both parents were born in Guatemala, in a tiny town without running water. Neither had finished school past high school. Survival had shaped them — resourceful, strong, frugal. They valued every penny, every honest hour of work. Their mother, the oldest of three, had started working as a child after her father died from untreated tuberculosis. Mariana's paternal grandfather had met a similar end — a hard worker consumed by alcohol after losing his wife, dead from cirrhosis.

Every Christmas, the stories would resurface. Her father would dedicate a mass for the departed. Mariana had always listened with reverence. Her own discipline — her focus in school and sports — was a way of saying *thank you*. The family had come to the U.S. when she was ten. Vanessa was only six. Mariana remembered Guatemala — the mountains, the sounds, the language.

And now... here they were.

————————

A cold, biting sensation crept up Richey's spine, dragging him from the depths of sleep.

"Aaah!" he shouted, jolting upright.

"I've been yelling for you to get up, boy," his father barked from the doorway.

Richey's back was soaked. Ice cubes clung to the sheet. He groaned. He didn't need to look — he already knew what had happened.

Classic Dad.

Water, ice, yelling. Pranks, he called them. But they weren't funny. They were little games wrapped in malice. His dad had always believed a man had to be tough, stoic, cold — and Richey never quite measured up.

His mother had left when he was four. She'd remarried and built a new life on the East Coast, with a new family. They spoke maybe once a year. Richey didn't blame her for leaving — not really. But it meant he was stuck here. Trapped.

He still remembered the scent of her perfume—a light vanilla scent that lingered on his clothes long after she hugged him goodbye for the last time. Sometimes, late at night, he wondered if things might have been different if she'd stayed. He'd once overheard his father muttering about how she couldn't handle the pressure, how she ran away instead of facing the reality. Deep down, Richey always feared he was the reality she couldn't face.

He pulled on the jeans from yesterday, stiff and creased from the floor. He sniffed a couple shirts until one passed the smell test. No time or energy to care about fashion. He shuffled toward the kitchen, rubbing his eyes.

Frozen waffles. Two of them. Into the toaster.

"Breakfast of champions," he muttered to himself with a dry smile.

From the living room came his father's voice — louder this time.

"You better be grateful. I oughta be charging you rent already. If your damn mother hadn't cleaned me out, we wouldn't even be in this dump."

Richey didn't answer. He never did. He sat at the kitchen counter and ate his waffles in silence, chewing mechanically.

He knew his dad blamed his mom for everything — for the divorce, the house, the bills. But deep down, Richey knew better. He'd lived with the man long enough to know just how far his temper could stretch. His dad had worked as a machinist for over twenty years, a proud union man — worked hard, drank harder. Richey couldn't remember a single night he hadn't stumbled through the door reeking of whiskey and resentment.

There hadn't been a woman's voice in the house for a long time. Richey had grown up around yelling and silence — never softness. Women, to him, were a foreign language. He didn't know how to speak to them, how to read them. Most of the time, he just tried to stay out of their way.

He was an "A" student. A second-string quarterback. And he knew his only shot out of this house was through grades — or maybe a scholarship. He didn't know which yet. But it had to be one of them.

"Hurry up before you're late," his father grunted. "I don't wanna hear from another damn teacher."

Richey grabbed his backpack and his gear bag. He didn't respond. There was no point. His dad was probably still half-drunk from the night before. Or hungover. Or both.

He rolled his bike out of the cluttered garage. The air outside was cool, the sky pale and quiet. Morning rides were his favorite part of the day — his only peace. The wind tousled his dirty blond hair as he coasted down the street. Football had shaped his tall, lean frame. He'd hit a growth spurt recently, and the faint stubble on his chin made him look older. Sometimes, on these rides, he let himself dream: college, a job, maybe a girl who didn't flinch when he spoke.

By the time he reached the school, his thoughts had wandered far from his house. Other juniors and seniors passed by in cars and on motorcycles, laughing, idling at the curb. Richey watched them briefly, then pulled into the bike rack and locked up.

Daniel was already waiting by the tree near the entrance.

"Wassup, Rich."

"Hey, D."

They bumped fists and started walking.

Richey didn't know much about his extended family. His father never talked about the past — never mentioned his own parents. That silence was thick, heavy. It made Richey wonder if maybe it was pain, or shame, that kept it sealed off. So he invented stories to fill in the blanks. Whole lives imagined in quiet moments.

His mom had been more open. Her parents were Ukrainian immigrants, she'd said, fleeing war, scraping a life together out west. Richey had three half-siblings now. He'd met them as a kid and once more a few years ago. They looked happy. Normal. And he sometimes wondered — what did they have that he didn't? Was something wrong with him? Was he broken from the start?

Daniel was the only person he really talked to. His family owned a Vietnamese restaurant downtown. He was easygoing, smart, and fast — literally. Ran track as his main sport, usually placed top three, but also played receiver on the football team with Richey. His speed made him valuable in both sports. He wore his hair in a tight samurai bun, which Richey thought looked ridiculous, but he kept that opinion to himself. Daniel probably thought the same thing about his shaggy hair. Sometimes, Daniel talked about his older brother, Andrew — successful, confident, already enrolled at the Univerity of Texas on a full academic scholarship. Daniel joked openly about how impossible it was to compete with that, but Richey noticed the slight tightness in

Daniel's voice whenever Andrew was mentioned. It explained Daniel's drive—why he pushed himself so hard in track, in class, even socially. Beneath the jokes and easy smiles, Daniel felt a pressure too: quieter, subtler, but no less real.

"Hey, what are you doing after school?" Daniel asked.

"I dunno. Probably just Netflix and Xbox."

"I'm gonna check out the swim meet. It's supposed to be a big deal."

"I've got practice, but I'll hit you up after."

"Cool. Catch you later."

Daniel veered off toward his homeroom, and Richey headed to his own. At his locker, he grabbed his books for first period. He didn't even remember what was on the quiz today. He wasn't too worried. He had decent grades, and he usually did well just by paying attention in class.

Not that studying was encouraged at home.

His dad used to make fun of him whenever he tried to read. Said it wouldn't pay the bills. Called him a nerd. A wimp. Said "books are for losers" between swigs of warm beer. At some point, Richey stopped trying to argue. He'd just sneak study time at school or the library.

He worked part-time to cover some bills and have a little spending money. Asking his dad for twenty bucks for a movie or bowling night was pointless. Most of the time, it turned into a lecture about rent.

He hated that place.

And more than anything, he couldn't wait to leave.

1st Period Hallway Encounter

As Mariana and the girls made their way toward homeroom, a familiar raspy voice echoed across the hallway.

"Hey, Mariana!"

She turned and smiled. "Hi, Coach Riley! How are you?"

"I'm good. You ready for Regionals? Did you get enough sleep?"

Coach Riley always meant well. His tone could be gruff, and his frustration sometimes got the better of him, but his heart was in the right place.

"Yes, Coach. I feel good," she replied.

"That's what I like to hear," he said. "We need that win today. It could really help with that scholarship you've been talking about."

"I know, Coach. I'm going to do my best."

Before he could say more, a loud commotion erupted near the boys' locker room.

"I'll see you later, Mariana," he said, already jogging off to investigate.

The butterflies stirred in her stomach again. She loved swimming — not just the competition, but the solitude. The silence underwater. The control. There was something about the rhythmic breath, the graceful strokes, the gliding weightlessness that made her feel free.

"Come on, Mariana, we're gonna be late," Jackie said, grabbing her hand. "You don't want a detention and miss the competition."

They hurried past the rows of bright red lockers — Memorial High's colors were impossible to miss. The school was huge, over 2,500 students. Between classes, it felt like a tidal wave of bodies shifting and spilling into every hallway and stairwell. It was easy to disappear here. Easy to feel small.

Mariana had seen plenty during her years at Memorial. Kids vaping in the bathrooms. Others sneaking drinks in the corners not covered by cameras. She sometimes wondered what it would feel like — to rebel, even a little. But her parents had drilled the dangers of drugs into her early and often. They were the kind of parents who valued honesty above all — punishments were always lighter if you told the truth up front.

She loved them for that. But lately, every conversation seemed to spiral into hour-long lectures. It was starting to wear her down. She had begun keeping more to herself — not out of secrecy, but out of self-preservation. They wouldn't understand. Not the questions she was starting to have. About her future. About boys. About who she wanted to be — and not just what they wanted her to become.

Inside homeroom, Mrs. Kowalowski was already at her desk. She was a sturdy woman with cropped white hair and thick glasses that covered most of her face. Her sneakers squeaked faintly as she moved, always the same comfortable wardrobe on rotation. A widow for years now, she often blamed the Navy for her husband's death — he had served on one of the first nuclear submarines. Mariana had heard the story many times.

She took her usual seat by the window, third row back. As she pulled out her notes, she felt calm again. She had studied. Her grade was solid. This was just another checkpoint.

The classroom was old-school. A whiteboard at the front. No smart boards, no clicker-based quizzes. Just an overhead projector, the same kind teachers had used decades ago. But somehow, it fit Mrs. Kowalowski. She was sharp, knew her material, and never needed tech support.

First period was the same as homeroom, which Mariana didn't mind. She zoned out during the morning chatter, letting her eyes drift to the field outside. Overcast skies. Her favorite. A few students were running drills during P.E., and she found comfort in watching them move across the track. The diversity at Memorial High was its own kind of beauty — so many lives, backgrounds, and stories packed into the same building.

"Mariana?" came the voice from the front.

She blinked. "Here," she answered quickly.

The classroom had filled up while she was daydreaming. She glanced down and reviewed her notes one last time. A few others had first period with her, but the class was mostly quiet.

The bell rang — loud and sharp. After all these years, it still made her jump.

"Hey, Mariana," Stephanie whispered. "You ready for this?"

"I'm not too worried," Mariana said. "Did you not study?"

"Ugh, no," Stephanie said with a sly grin. "My boyfriend came over last night. We had some... quality time."

Mariana gave a half-smile, shaking her head. Out of the corner of her eye, she noticed him.

Richey.

Dirty blond hair, slouched walk, hands in his hoodie pocket. He sat behind her in first period. She hadn't paid him much attention before — or maybe she had, quietly. Stephanie followed her gaze and raised an eyebrow. She remembered seeing him once watching her swim practice from the bleachers, his expression thoughtful rather than leering like some boys. She'd wondered then what he was thinking.

"You should talk to him."

"And say what?" Mariana whispered back.

"I dunno... 'Hey, how are you? I think you're cute. Want to hang out sometime?'" Stephanie teased, grinning wider now.

"I'm not saying any of that," Mariana said quickly, her cheeks warming. "If he wants to talk to me, he can talk to me."

As if on cue, Richey walked up and took his seat behind her. He glanced at them briefly. He always noticed the quiet girl who sat in front of him.

"Stephanie, stop," Mariana muttered, waving her off. "You're embarrassing me."

Stephanie giggled and went back to her seat. Richey settled in behind Mariana. She kept her eyes forward, but she could feel his presence now more than ever. They had gone to the same middle school, hadn't they? How had she never really noticed him before?

She'd never had a boyfriend. Never had the time. Sports and school had always filled her days — to her parents' delight, of course. She vaguely remembered seeing Richey around since middle school, occasionally catching him watching her in class or at swim meets, but they'd never really spoken."

"Alright, everybody. Take your seats and pipe down," came Mrs. Kowalowski's voice, cutting through the chatter.

She began roll call in alphabetical order.

"Richard?"

"Here!" Richey replied from behind her.

"Mariana?"

"Here," she answered.

Mrs. Kowalowski was known for calling out anyone who didn't respond fast enough. Mariana wasn't going to test her patience.

The teacher stood, a stack of papers in hand.

"Alright folks. Clear your desks — pen or pencil only."

Just then, a light tap on her shoulder.

"'Hey, Marian -- you got an extra pen I can borrow?' She turned slightly, startled by the whisper. It was rare for him to initiate conversation, though she'd noticed his glances before."

"Uh, yeah. Hold on."

She rummaged through her pencil bag and passed one back to him.

"Here you go, Richard."

"Please — call me Richey. Richard's my dad's name... and he's way too serious for me."

His voice cracked slightly as he said it. He flushed red immediately. That damn voice — always betraying him at the worst times. Why didn't it crack when he talked to Daniel or his dad? Why only now?

Mariana chuckled. "You got it, Richey."

She turned back, smiling to herself. There was something about him. Something different today. Taller. More grounded. Maybe she'd just never really looked before. He always seemed like a loner — never at parties or school events. Just there. Quiet. Watching.

Mrs. Kowalowski walked through the rows, handing out the quiz: multiple choice, short answer, and true/false. Nothing she wasn't prepared for.

Mariana finished early, as usual. She set her pencil down and leaned back, letting her gaze drift to the field outside again.

The rest of the class scratched away, heads down, time ticking on.

3rd Period Locker Room News

"Yo, Rich — wait up!" came Daniel's voice from behind.

Richey slowed his pace, letting his friend catch up. They had a habit of linking up before third period — the walk was sort of a ritual. Usually, they talked about games, practice, or whatever show they were binging.

They'd known each other since elementary school, but the friendship truly began in fourth grade. Richey still remembered the day like it was branded into his bones... Patrick Langley had been shoving Daniel around near the bike racks... Richey charged Patrick, pushed him with everything he had... Daniel came over every day that week with comic books and orange soda. Richey never forgot it.

"Did you hear what happened to Jimmy?" Daniel asked, keeping his voice low.

Richey raised an eyebrow. "You mean yesterday? Yeah, I saw him take a hit, but didn't think it was serious. Trainers took him out."

Daniel nodded grimly. "Yeah. He blew out his ACL. He's done for the season."

Richey froze mid-step.

His stomach dropped. His thoughts scrambled. That meant...

He was starting.

Next Saturday.

Coach was going to be on him nonstop. He'd have to review every play, memorize every call. His heart began to race. His chest tightened. He wasn't ready.

Was he?

Was he really good enough to lead the team? To step in for Jimmy?

Daniel, catching the shift in Richey's expression, clapped a hand on his shoulder.

"Rich, breathe. Jimmy's gonna be alright — he's got doctors for that. You need to focus on you now. Big game coming. This is your shot."

"Thanks, man. I just... I want to play well — for the team, for the school," Richey said, trying to steady himself.

"You will. Don't worry," Daniel said with a grin. "And hey — now you're the main star. Might even catch some attention from the girls, too."

He nudged Richey playfully.

Richey hadn't even thought of that. Jimmy had always been the guy — the one with the girls hanging on his arm, the charm, the image. Now Richey was in that spotlight.

But he wasn't Jimmy. And he didn't want to be. Their team was undefeated this year. Just two more games before Regionals — and maybe, finally, State. Last year, they'd lost in the final round. That sting still lingered.

This year had to be different.

Richey dreamed of a scholarship. Not the NFL — that was never the goal — but a good university. A real future. A ticket out.

Something his father would never understand.

He didn't let that thought linger. Not today.

They walked into third period calculus together. The whispers had already started. Jimmy's injury was all anyone could talk about. Richey could feel the eyes — curious, speculative, even admiring. He didn't mind that.

What he *did* mind was who he shared this class with.

A couple senior linemen were already sprawled in the back. Richey was used to the daily ritual — the jokes, the jabs, the digs. His shaggy hair. His thrift store sneakers. The fact he biked to school. And of course, the nickname.

"Look what the poverty bus dragged in today," Chad sneered from his desk.

Team center. Loud, cocky, and twice Richey's size.

"So what, you think you're better than Jimmy now? Richey Broke," he added with a smirk.

Richey said nothing. He wasn't about to get into it — not with Chad. He'd need the guy to block for him on Saturday.

"I'm gonna talk to Coach," Chad went on. "Make sure your scrawny ass doesn't see a single snap."

Richey exhaled through his nose. Thought carefully. Then calmly asked:

"You still waiting on that Auburn scholarship, Chad?"

Chad blinked. That clearly threw him.

"And what the hell's it to you?" he snapped, his voice rising.

"I'm your best shot to get there now," Richey said evenly. "I want this as bad as you do. This is my way out."

He looked Chad square in the eyes, expression flat but firm.

"You don't have to like me. Hell, you don't even have to talk to me. But you *will* block your ass off for me — because I'll be out there giving everything I've got for this team."

The room went quiet.

Chad stared at him. Then his shoulders dropped slightly.

"Dammit, Richey Broke... you're right."

He pointed a thick finger at him. "But so help me God, if you don't come out swinging, me and the boys will *end* you."

Richey straightened his back. "You let me worry about that. Just make sure your boys handle business on their end."

A beat passed. Then Chad cracked half a grin and sat back down.

Richey turned — and realized the whole class was watching. He hadn't meant to make a scene, but the weight of what just happened settled on him like armor.

He'd stood his ground. He'd gotten through to Chad.

That mattered.

Daniel sat nearby, mouth slightly open. Richey caught his expression and grinned.

At least he'd made an impression.

Moments later, the class dissolved back into routine — the glow of phone screens, the hum of Snapchat videos and Instagram scrolls. But Richey stayed still for a moment, breathing it in.

This moment felt... different.

He thought about his phone — or lack thereof. While everyone else had the latest iPhones, he still used an old flip phone. It was a hand-me-down from his uncle. No apps. No camera. Just texts and calls.

He kind of liked that.

It wasn't flashy. But it worked.

Just like him.

The period bell rang, loud and final, cutting through the air. The last of the stragglers stumbled in.

Mr. Peters entered right behind them, setting his coffee on the desk.

"Settle down, everyone," he called out. "Let's get started. Today we're talking Riemann Sums — open to page 437."

He scanned the room.

"Mr. Richard," he said, glancing over his glasses, "would you do us the honor?"

Richey smirked and flipped open his book.

"Sure thing, Mr. P."

5th Period Invitation

Mariana had packed her usual modest lunch: a sandwich, a handful of grapes, and a snack-sized bag of Cheetos. Normally, she would've added a cookie or some chips, but she'd been in a rush that morning. Her stomach was already starting to rumble, and she knew it would only get worse by the time the swim meet rolled around.

I'll grab something else before fifth period, she thought.

But before she could get up, the bell rang.

"Alright, see you guys later," Mariana said, rising and heading for the trash can.

"Okay, Captain! See you after school," one of the girls called.

"Later, Mari," came from another table.

The swim team always sat together. It wasn't a rule, exactly — more of an unspoken agreement. Unity mattered. Over time, other cliques followed suit: football players, soccer kids, band members. Even the so-called outcasts — the loners, stoners, and emos — formed their own islands of familiarity during the social chaos of high school lunch.

Mariana had always found this fascinating — the way people who claimed not to care about social rules still formed patterns of their own. She never understood the irony: if you truly wanted to blend in, wouldn't you just... conform?

But she didn't have time to overthink it. The next bell rang.

She merged into the wave of students flooding the hallway,

everyone moving in a barely controlled chaos, like atoms scattering toward their assigned orbits. She let herself drift toward English class.

"Hey! Mariana, wait up!" called a voice behind her.

Jackie jogged forward, grabbing Mariana's arm with theatrical excitement.

"You're not gonna believe this," she whispered, eyes glowing. "My parents are stuck in Boston. Their flight's delayed — they won't be back until tomorrow afternoon!"

Jackie paused briefly, her excitement flickering for just an instant. Mariana caught the sudden change, the quick shift from excitement to something more guarded.

'Honestly, they probably prefer it this way,' Jackie muttered, her voice softer now. 'I swear they'd rather send money than spend time. It's like every trip, every excuse—it's always the same. So predictable it's almost funny.' Jackie forced a quick laugh, but her eyes didn't join in.

Mariana recognized that look: a deep-seated bitterness Jackie usually hid behind humor or drama.

Mariana blinked. "Okay... why are you telling me this?"

Then it hit her.

The party.

In the rush of the day, the meet, the homework, she'd forgotten completely. But now she saw it — the gears turning in Jackie's head. That wild glint in her eyes. This was no casual sleepover anymore.

"So... what are you planning?" Mariana asked warily.

Jackie leaned in like she was sharing state secrets.

"You know how it was just supposed to be a few friends spending the night? Well, I ran into Daniel before lunch. Told him the situation. He says he has a cousin who's over twenty-one. And guess what? He's down to buy us stuff — drinks, whatever — as long as he and a few of his guys can come too."

Mariana's stomach turned — not from fear, but from the sheer weight of what Jackie was suggesting. This wasn't the deal she'd made with her mom. Her parents had only agreed because Jackie's parents were supposed to supervise. Now? It was a full-blown party in the making.

Jackie was practically bouncing. "This is going to be *legendary*! Everyone's gonna be talking about it Monday. Who came. Who didn't. Who got left out. It's like... social Darwinism in real time."

Mariana noticed a slight edge to Jackie's enthusiasm, the way her eyes darted nervously even as she smiled. It wasn't the first time she'd seen this side of Jackie—the intense swings between excitement and anxiety, the desperate need for validation through social success.

Mariana pulled her aside before they entered the classroom.

"What are we going to tell my mom? She wants to call and talk to me before bed. She'll hear the music. The voices. She's not going to buy it."

Jackie rolled her eyes, but softened her voice. "Don't stress. We'll just go in my parents' room. You take the call from there — it'll be quiet. She won't suspect anything."

Mariana didn't respond immediately. Her pulse was quickening.

Her parents would *never* be okay with this. And if they found out afterward? The trust would collapse. But there was something else rising inside her now — something she wasn't used to listening to.

Curiosity. Longing.

Being part of an immigrant family came with its own gravity. Her parents had no support when they moved to the U.S. from Guatemala — no cousins, no grandparents, no safety net. Just each other, and later, their daughters. They'd grown up in a small rural town, three hours from Guatemala City, and carried those beliefs with them: caution, modesty, faith, tradition.

Mariana had heard it all. The lectures about "American excess." The warnings about drinking, boys, parties, rebellion. The endless comparisons to her cousins who were *more respectful*. And underneath all of it — fear.

They meant well. But their love was wrapped in barbed wire.

And lately... it was wearing her down.

She couldn't help it. When other girls at school talked about sleepovers, parties, dances, all-nighters — she felt something gnawing inside her. A low, persistent ache. She wanted to know what it felt like to dance in a living room with friends and music and sweat. To laugh at things her parents wouldn't understand. To make mistakes. To be a little reckless. Just once.

The past year had been rough. More fights. More tension. Every weekend it felt like something came up that she wasn't allowed to attend. It wasn't fair.

And now... here was this moment. Maybe her only chance.

Her thoughts turned to Vanessa. She'd need to talk to her sister before the meet — make sure she didn't say anything, didn't blow this up. Vanessa could keep a secret. Especially if there was a little incentive involved.

Mariana and Vanessa were close. Not perfect — they fought like any sisters close in age — but there was trust there. And Mariana would need her.

The bell rang again, snapping her out of the spiral. She looked around and realized she was already seated. Jackie had moved on, talking animatedly to another group.

"Take your seats, everyone," came Ms. Velazquez's calm voice from the front.

"I hope you all had a chance to review the assignment and finish your papers. I'll be collecting them after class."

Mariana exhaled.

The meet. The quiz. The party. Her mom's call. Vanessa. Jackie. The plan.

She had a long day ahead.

And no idea how it was going to end.

8th Period Pressure Building

This has been one wild day, Richey thought, weaving through the crowded hallway between classes.

He'd been stopped three times already — once by a lineman, once by a girl from his Spanish class, and once by the kid who sat behind him in Algebra but never talked before. Everyone wanted to know the same thing.

"Is Jimmy really out?"

"Are you playing?"

"Can you handle it?"

Some voices came with genuine encouragement. Others carried that sarcastic sting — not quite bullying, not quite support. Just enough to make him feel exposed.

More people were looking at him now. Some whispered. A few smirked. A cluster of girls near the vending machine actually giggled as he walked past, eyes trailing after him.

This is definitely new, he thought, almost amused. *This is something I could get used to.*

But the thought didn't sit comfortably for long. Because he knew — **he knew** — that if he weren't second-string quarterback, if he weren't suddenly the "next guy up," most of these people wouldn't even look at him.

And that truth lingered in the back of his mind like a splinter.

They don't care about me. They care about the position.

That creeping pressure returned — a familiar heaviness that pressed against his chest, coiling around his ribs. What if he failed? What if he couldn't perform? What if this was just one more chance life handed him so it could rip it away again?

You're jumping before you've even reached the gap, moron, came his father's voice in his head, gruff and condescending.

It wasn't advice. It was mockery disguised as wisdom. Still, it worked. He pushed the anxiety down.

"Richey! Hold up, man!"

Daniel's voice broke through the fog. Richey turned to see his best friend hustling to catch up, his usual backpack slung one-armed across his shoulder.

"What now?" Richey asked, sensing the buzz in Daniel's tone.

"Dude. *Today* is gonna get nuts," Daniel said, barely able to contain himself. "Okay, so you remember my cousin Steven, right? Tatted-up guy from the family barbecue last year?"

"Yeah. Offered me a joint before I even stepped inside."

"Exactly!" Daniel laughed. "Well, get this. I'm talking to Jackie, right? She tells me her parents are stuck in Boston until tomorrow. And she wants to throw a *real* party."

Richey's eyebrows lifted. "Like... what kind of real?"

"Like, legit. Not just girls in pajamas eating popcorn. She wants drinks. Maybe more. And guess who she asked for help?"

"Oh God. You?"

"Yes, me! I texted Steven. Told him what was up. He's cool with bringing booze — maybe even some molly, some pills, whatever. As long as he can bring a couple of his guys."

"And you think that's a good idea?"

Daniel shrugged. "Dude, it's fine. I told him not to bring anyone sketchy. Just chill guys. We'll keep it under control."

Richey shook his head. "You sure Jackie's ready for that kind of scene?"

"Honestly? No idea. But it's happening." Daniel grinned. "Anyway, don't worry about that. You've got enough going on. Just focus on practice and get ready to *own* next weekend."

He wasn't wrong.

Still, Richey couldn't shake the image of Jackie's living room filled with strangers and red solo cups. The thought made him anxious — and oddly intrigued.

He hadn't been to a real party before.

Most of his weekends involved solo workouts, game replays, or just lying on his bed with a book and his beat-up headphones. It wasn't that he didn't want fun. It was just... complicated.

Daniel, though, had always been different. Charismatic. Fast-talking. And loyal — which counted more than anything else.

They'd known each other since elementary school, but the friendship truly began in fourth grade. Richey still remembered the day like it was branded into his bones.

Patrick Langley had been shoving Daniel around near the bike racks. No one else had stepped in. But something in Richey had snapped. He charged Patrick, pushed him with everything he had, and watched him crash backward onto the pavement.

Seventeen stitches. One ambulance. A week-long suspension.

But also: his first real friend.

Daniel came over every day that week with comic books and orange soda. Richey never forgot it. Even his father, surprisingly, hadn't punished him.

"Good," he'd said. "You showed backbone. That little punk had it coming."

It was one of the rare moments Richey felt... seen.

The memory faded as they arrived outside eighth period — history with Mr. Zambrano, the longest stretch of the day. The class Richey dreaded.

The subject just didn't stick. Wars, treaties, civilizations — all of it blurred into meaningless dates and names. He didn't understand why the past mattered so much.

Why live in yesterday when today is hard enough?

That was the real reason he struggled with history. It reminded him of his own — one he worked hard to forget. Nights alone. Doors slammed. Bruises, both visible and not. Things better buried.

The final bell rang out, jarring him from the spiral.

As they slid into their seats, Daniel leaned over. "So? You coming tonight?"

Richey hesitated.

"To the party, man," Daniel prompted. "Come after practice. We'll roll over together. Bring something decent to wear — not one of those grandpa tees."

"I don't know..." Richey sighed. "I can't stay out late. You know I've got the game next Saturday. I need to be on point."

"You'll be fine," Daniel waved him off. "You need to *loosen up* a little. You've got a starting spot now — live a little!"

Richey wasn't so sure. But Daniel's grin was infectious.

"Fine," he said. "But I'm not staying long."

"That's my boy. Bring your first-string energy."

Richey cracked a smile, but inside, the anxiety twisted again.

Steven—Daniel's cousin had always seemed like trouble. The kind of guy who had too many stories and not enough accountability. Tattoos. Muscle car. Girlfriends in every town. No job anyone could name.

And yet, Daniel idolized him.

Richey just wanted to stay out of trouble. No screw-ups. Not now. Not when it mattered.

Opportunities didn't come around often. Not for him. Not for people like him. He had learned early on that **life didn't give handouts** — it gave you just enough rope to hang your hopes with.

And then pulled it back.

The screech of chairs echoed as the final students sat.

Mr. Zambrano strolled in, coffee in one hand, stack of folders in the other. His voice was dry as gravel but always sharp.

"Alright, let's get started, people. Last class of the day. I know half of you are already halfway into weekend mode, but try to keep your brains inside your skulls for forty-five more minutes."

A few students chuckled.

"And if I catch anyone on their phones, I'm confiscating them and filling the gallery with embarrassing selfies. Trust me, your Snap scores won't survive the damage."

Richey smirked. He liked Zambrano. Not the subject — but the man. He had presence. Humor. He didn't pretend to be anyone else.

"Open your books to chapter fifteen," Zambrano continued. "We're covering Reconstruction today — a.k.a., the part where America screws up the aftermath of the Civil War."

As papers rustled and books opened, Richey allowed himself a deep breath.

The game. The party. The pressure. The weight of everything still ahead.

Just get through today, he told himself.

Then tomorrow... everything changes.

Warming Up

The final bell rang — sharp, metallic, and unrelenting.

As if released from a cage, students jumped to their feet, conversations spilling into the hallway with the flood of backpacks and shuffled sneakers. Normally, Mariana felt a small wave of relief at this moment — the end of another day, the beginning of the weekend. But today, the feeling didn't come.

Today was different.

There was no sigh of closure, no breath of ease. Only the quickening thud of her heart and a creeping, constant pressure she couldn't quite shake. The next few hours weren't just about winning or losing — they could shape her future.

She made her way to her locker, twisting the dial with practiced fingers. The hallway was thinning, students peeling off in every direction. Some laughing, others already talking about party plans or weekend hangouts. Mariana felt like she was walking underwater, her mind split between the meet... and Jackie's party.

She shoved her books into the locker and slammed it shut. She wouldn't need them this weekend. Her hand lingered on the lock a moment longer, as if pausing there might delay the decisions still ahead.

Where was Jackie? Normally they'd meet here and walk together. But Mariana remembered Daniel's involvement — and Jackie's new plans. Probably busy securing her chaos.

She didn't want to be involved in *that* part of it.

The idea of no parental supervision already had her on edge. She still hadn't figured out what she was going to tell her mom. Maybe she could get Vanessa to stall her during the phone call, keep things sounding normal. Her heart beat faster just thinking about it.

Focus, Mariana. One thing at a time.

She turned down the corridor and headed toward the gym and pool complex. The school had invested heavily in its athletic facilities a few years back, right before she started high school. The aquatic center was beautiful — regulation lanes, professional-grade tiles, high-grade diving boards, and bleachers that could hold nearly a thousand. It was part of what made Memorial High such a formidable name in state swimming. That reputation was something Mariana wore like armor.

On the way toward the entrance, she spotted Vanessa cutting through the crowd, her backpack bouncing against her hip. She had that look — wide grin, eyes gleaming like she already knew something.

"Mariana!" she called, jogging over. "Is it true there's a party tonight?"

Mariana blinked. "What? How did you—?"

Vanessa smirked. "So it *is* true. I heard people whispering about it in third period. And I *knew* you'd be going. You're staying at Jackie's, right?"

Mariana hesitated, glancing around. "Yes, but you can't tell Mom. Please. I mean it."

"Oh, I won't," Vanessa said with faux innocence. "But... it's gonna cost you."

Mariana groaned. "Seriously?"

Vanessa crossed her arms, smirk widening. "Let me use your nice makeup. The fancy one. For the rest of the year."

"Absolutely not! Do you know how expensive that stuff is?"

"Three months, then. Final offer."

Mariana sighed in frustration. "Fine. Three months. You're a little extortionist, you know that?"

"Call it sisterly insurance," Vanessa said smugly. "You *are* asking me to lie to Mom. That's a felony in our house."

"I've covered for you a dozen times—"

"Yeah, but this is big, and you *know* it."

Mariana rolled her eyes but couldn't help smiling a little. "Alright. Deal."

They paused near the breezeway where students were dispersing. For all their petty fights and teasing, their bond was solid. Closer in age, they understood each other more than their parents often could.

"You coming with Mom later?" Mariana asked.

Vanessa's face fell slightly. "I don't know about Dad. You know how he is."

"Yeah... don't hold your breath," Mariana said quietly.

Vanessa reached out and squeezed her arm. "But *I'll* be there. Screaming your name and everything."

"Thanks."

They hugged quickly — neither the overly sentimental type — and then separated, each stepping back into their roles: younger sister, older sister, athlete, student.

Mariana continued toward the aquatic center, cutting across the overhead bridge that split the campus. The school was massive — the football fields and soccer stadium were on the far end, disconnected from the academic buildings. Being in a crowded metro area like Houston meant the school had grown in patches, constantly expanding upward or outward in awkward bursts. Still, she didn't mind the walk.

It gave her time to think.

Each step brought a deeper awareness of the weight pressing on her chest — not from fear, but from purpose. Everything she'd done — the 6 a.m. practices, the dietary sacrifices, the discipline — all of it was leading here. To this meet. This moment. Her chance to leave a mark, maybe even get noticed.

This is it, she thought. *Validation. It all has to count.*

As she neared the main entrance, she could hear Coach Riley's voice from the other side — barking orders, directing warmups, his trademark rasp cutting through the humid air.

She paused.

She could skip the front entrance, take the back hallway, avoid the inevitable pep talk she didn't feel ready for.

But no. Better to face it now than postpone the inevitable.

She squared her shoulders and pushed through the door.

"Mariana! Where've you been?" Coach Riley called immediately, not waiting for an answer. "Everyone's already changing. Get that suit on and get in the water. Let's warm up — come on now!"

"Yes, Coach!" Mariana responded automatically.

That was... strange. No speech. No deep motivational stare. Just orders. Direct. Brisk. Coach Riley *never* skipped the pre-meet pep talk, especially not with her.

She walked into the locker room, and the tension hit her like a wall.

Everyone was already changing — half-suits on, towels draped over shoulders, goggles clicking into place.

"Whoa, did I miss something?" Mariana asked, setting her bag down. "Coach is on edge."

Stephanie turned from the mirror, mid-bun twist. "You're telling me. He gave us this whole speech already — about commitment, doing our best, and not worrying about the outcome."

Mariana frowned. "Since when does he not care about the outcome?"

"That's what I said!" Stephanie whispered. "But I asked my mom after lunch... and she told me something."

"What?"

"There are recruiters here."

Mariana stopped cold.

"What kind of recruiters?"

"College recruiters. From two big schools. They're watching today."

The world tilted.

A flush rose in Mariana's neck. Her limbs felt light, like they might detach. Her breathing slowed. That knot in her chest twisted, and for a second, she thought she might be sick.

"Mariana? Are you okay?" Stephanie asked, voice faint, distant.

Mariana blinked, nodded. "Yeah. Just... didn't expect that."

She took a deep breath, feeling the weight of the moment settle like a stone in her stomach.

This was no longer just a meet.

This was a future.

She looked around at her teammates — girls adjusting straps, shaking out nerves, wiping fogged lenses. They were just as tense. Probably just as scared.

They need to see strength, she thought. *They need a captain right now.*

She clapped her hands together, drawing the room's attention.

"Alright, listen up," she said, loud and clear. "I know we're all feeling it. But we've trained for this. We've *earned* this. Doesn't matter who's out there — recruiters, scouts, Coach Riley's grandma — we go in that pool and give everything we've got."

Heads turned. Bodies shifted.

"I'm nervous too," Mariana admitted. "But we let the water do the talking tonight. Let's show Cypress High why we're Memorial. Let's show them what *we* do."

A cheer erupted through the locker room, and for the first time all day, Mariana felt that flutter in her chest transform — not fear, but energy. Drive.

This was her moment.

She turned and began changing quickly. Her suit was top-tier, specially designed for competition — expensive, streamlined, practically sculpted. Her parents had made sacrifices to afford it. She thought about their overtime hours, their cautious budgeting, the other things they'd said no to just to make this one *yes* happen.

She wouldn't let that go to waste.

She finished her routine, adjusting her goggles, double-checking the tightness of her straps. She grabbed two towels from the rack and slung them over her arm.

As she stepped out of the locker room and toward the pool deck, the humid air and sharp scent of chlorine met her like a wall.

The stands were already filling. The water gleamed beneath the stadium lights.

Mariana stood at the edge of the pool.

Ready.

The Meet

The stands were packed.

The roar of voices echoed like waves crashing against concrete. Every bleacher seat in the Natatorium was filled, and people spilled over onto the walkways and corners of the tiled perimeter, leaning against railings, standing on tiptoe. Mariana had never seen it this full. Not even at last year's semifinals.

There were banners from unfamiliar schools — teams from all over the state, some of which she'd never even heard of before. Strangers in different colored tracksuits walked past her like quiet shadows, their faces sharp with focus.

The energy was electric.

Mariana stood at the entrance of the pool deck, towel wrapped around her shoulders, eyes scanning the sea of faces. The buzzing hum of voices blurred together into something almost physical — like the water, it surrounded her, carried her, pressed against her chest.

Then she saw them.

Her mom, sitting in the third row from the front, straight-backed and bright-eyed. Her sister Vanessa waved with both hands like she was trying to hail a helicopter. Their presence hit Mariana with a strange surge of gratitude and ache. She lifted her arm and waved back, forcing a smile.

And then the butterflies hit.

Not the small ones — the fluttering kind that tap lightly at your ribs. These were full-winged creatures crashing into her stomach, tightening her breath. Her throat constricted.

It's happening again.

Her breathing shortened. Her vision narrowed. The sounds around her became distant — muffled, like underwater echoes.

She recognized this.

Panic attacks. They never announced themselves. They just appeared. Creeping, squeezing, dragging her inward. Like a hand reaching up from beneath the surface to pull her under.

She blinked and focused on the tip of a nearby lifeguard's whistle. *Focus on one thing.* That's what Coach Riley had taught her.

She reached down and pressed her fingertips to the rough edge of the bleacher railing beside her. *Ground yourself.* Another one of his methods.

Then she began her breathing sequence.

In for four. Hold. Out for seven.

One... two... three... four.

Hold.

One... two... three... four... five... six... seven.

Again.

Gradually, the tightness in her chest eased. Her pulse slowed from the erratic drumbeat to a steadier rhythm. The echo faded. The world came back into focus. She took one last deep breath, steadying herself. There was no time to dwell, no room for hesitation—not now. Her family was watching, her coach was counting on her, and above all, she needed this victory to prove to herself that the sacrifices meant something. Gathering her resolve, Mariana straightened, pulled back her shoulders, and stepped forward, leaving fear at the water's edge.

Another battle won, she thought, exhaling.

She had never fully understood why the attacks happened. Sometimes they struck before competitions, sometimes in the middle of them. Once, years ago, she'd frozen mid-race — lost in her own body. It terrified her more than any loss ever could. The feeling of being *trapped* inside yourself, paralyzed and helpless, ran completely counter to everything she tried to be.

A sound cut through the fog — a voice. Her mother.

She looked up. Her mom was watching her closely, her expression soft but focused. She gave Mariana a small wave and a warm smile, the kind only a mother could give — full of history, exhaustion, and fierce love. Mariana smiled back.

She sees me, Mariana thought. *She knows.*

Her mom had always been there. The early morning drives. The soaked towels in the trunk. The quiet, faithful clapping from the stands even when Mariana came in second, or third, or last. She was a constant — a quiet fortress in Mariana's life.

The gratitude filled her lungs and pressed behind her eyes.

Mariana turned and made her way toward the locker room. She needed to suit up.

Inside, it was chaos. Steam clung to the mirrors. Girls elbowed for locker space. Towels slung over hooks. The tiled floor glistened with water and nerves.

There wasn't much space left, but she found a sliver near the far end and knelt to unzip her bag. Her hands trembled slightly.

She wasn't great at changing in front of others. It wasn't shame, exactly — just discomfort. She'd never liked the vulnerability of undressing in loud, fluorescent-lit rooms surrounded by bodies in motion.

But today, she was too focused to care.

She unzipped the sealed pouch that held her competition suit. It was sleek and black, compressive, built like armor. She hated putting it on — it took time and effort, inch by inch, stretch by stretch. It hugged her skin tightly, almost painfully so. But once it was on, she always felt different. Sharper. Tuned.

Like a blade instead of a girl.

She folded her clothes neatly, slid them into the locker, and took one last look in the mirror. She adjusted her straps, then her cap. No strands loose. Goggles ready. Joints warmed.

Let's do this.

She stepped out just in time to hear the booming voice of Coach Riley.

"Mariana! You're late. Warm-up pool. Twenty minutes. Go."

"Yes, Coach!" she called back, already moving.

The water welcomed her like an old friend — cold and biting, but familiar. She dove in without hesitation, body slicing through the surface like a blade.

The first moment beneath the water was always a kind of rebirth.

Silence. Suspension. Everything else — the crowd, the expectations, the pressure — melted away. Just the feel of her body and the current. That quiet space where her mind could let go.

She stayed under until her lungs ached, then surfaced with a clean, seamless stroke and transitioned into freestyle. Her form was tight, practiced. Elbows high. Reach long. Head low. She focused on the rhythm.

Pull. Over. Out. Pull. Over. Out.

Every motion was intentional. Every breath measured.

She passed the halfway mark. Spotted the tiled "T" signaling the wall. Prepped her turn.

The flip was fluid — legs tight, core tight, toes flexed. She pushed off with everything she had.

She had done this a thousand times. In this water. In this lane.

But today, everything felt magnified.

After a few more laps, Coach Riley waved her over. She climbed the ladder, water trailing down her legs in rivulets. Her arms buzzed — not with fatigue, but anticipation.

She towel-dried quickly and sat near her bag, stretching her arms, rotating her shoulders. She took another breath, then another.

But the thoughts were creeping in again.

Why do I do this to myself?

Why all this pressure? What's the point?

But she already knew.

Because this *mattered*. Because this was her shot. Because there were eyes in the crowd tonight that could shape her future.

"Mariana!" Coach Riley bellowed from across the deck. "You're up! Lane three, pool two! Get your butt on that stand!"

She nearly jumped out of her skin. How he managed to project over hundreds of people was a mystery.

Mariana stood quickly, drying her feet, pulling her goggles down tight. She took one last look at the crowd.

Her mother stood, hand pressed to her heart. Vanessa beside her, fists clenched, yelling something Mariana couldn't hear. That was enough.

Mariana stepped up onto the block.

The platform was wet and cold beneath her soles. The grip tape was peeling from years of wear. She adjusted her feet. Bent her knees. Found her balance.

She took one breath. Then another. The world shrank around her.

Let's get this done, she whispered to herself.

The whistle blew.

She dove.

Crossing the Bridge

The final bell rang.

It echoed through the halls like a signal flare, and within seconds the school came alive — lockers slamming, laughter bouncing off tile walls, sneakers scuffing linoleum. Richey pushed his chair back and slung his bag over his shoulder.

"Good luck out there, Richey," called Mr. Zambrano from behind his desk. "And remember — pet the sweaty stuff, forget the petty stuff."

Richey grinned, shaking his head. "Still don't know what that means, but thanks, Mr. Z."

"Wisdom is like bad chili," the teacher added, waving him off. "Burns now. Sits better later."

Richey stepped into the hallway, shoulders tight with anticipation. He didn't run. He didn't walk fast either. He just moved with purpose.

Every hallway felt louder than usual. Kids clumped in clusters, excited for the weekend. Some of them looked up and gave him a nod. A few even clapped him on the shoulder as he passed.

"Gonna light it up tomorrow, Broke!"

"QB1, baby!"

He wasn't used to it — this attention. It buzzed in his ears, a blend of expectation and disbelief. As he approached the glass doors that led to the bridge over Memorial Avenue — the one connecting the main building to the athletic complex — he felt the shift in energy.

He was no longer just a student. He was a symbol now. A gamble. A possible hero or disaster. And everyone had a stake in the outcome.

Outside, the air was thick with humidity. The sun hung low and hot, casting shadows through the chainlink fencing on either side of the pedestrian bridge. Beneath his feet, the cars zoomed past, indifferent to the pressure swelling inside him.

Halfway across the bridge, Richey spotted them — three coaches in polo shirts standing just past the front office. Their heads were huddled close, voices low, until one of them looked up and caught sight of him.

The man raised his hand, motioning him over. Coach Kenneck turned with that ever-present clipboard under one arm and squinted toward the bridge. Richey picked up his pace.

"Richard," Kenneck said when he approached. "How you feeling?"

Richey nodded. "I'm alright, Coach."

"You heard about Jimmy?"

"Yeah. Pretty much everyone at school knows. Sucks."

Coach Kenneck took a deep breath, as if choosing his words with care.

"Well, you know what this means."

Richey nodded again. "You need me to step up."

"That's putting it lightly. We've got two games left. One win takes us to Regionals. Two... and we're back at State."

Coach leaned in slightly. "You ready?"

"I am. And I want it, Coach. I'm not here to be Jimmy's backup anymore. I'm ready to run this team."

That was all Kenneck needed.

"Good. Get dressed. Field in ten."

"Yes, sir."

Richey took off for the field house, adrenaline already rushing to his fingertips. As he pushed open the heavy double doors, the scent hit him — sweat, old gear, and the unmistakable tang of ambition.

The weight room was already filled. Defensive players were finishing circuits, grunting under racks and clanking iron. All motion slowed when Richey walked in.

Heads turned.

Stares lingered.

A few whispers passed between players.

Richey didn't respond. He turned left down the hallway to the locker room, keeping his posture tight, controlled. His heart thudded louder than the noise behind him.

He reached his locker, dropped his bag, and began unfastening his belt. He was halfway into his gear when he felt a shadow behind him.

"Well, well," came Chad's voice — low, amused, and venom-laced. "If it isn't Richey *Broke*."

Richey didn't turn around.

He pulled his jersey from the locker, laid it across the bench, and began undoing his cleats.

"I'm talking to you, asswipe," Chad snarled.

A strong hand grabbed his arm and spun him around.

Richey came face-to-face with the senior center, flanked by two other linemen. Chad's shoulders were massive. His neck, barely visible beneath his helmet strap, looked like a brick wall.

But Richey didn't flinch.

"What?" he said, voice steady. "You gonna threaten me? Tell me if I mess up, you'll break my face? That everyone will hate me?"

Chad blinked — caught off-guard by the honesty.

"Yeah, you better believe—"

"Get out of my face, Chad."

Richey's voice rose, not in anger, but in command.

"I know what's on the line. I know what this team needs. But I need you to stop playing locker room tough guy and start playing like my blocker."

He looked around — saw the room had gone still. The entire offensive unit had paused mid-lace, mid-wrap, mid-laugh.

"I'm not Jimmy," Richey continued. "But I'm not scared either. I need this. You think I don't? This is my one shot. And I *will* take it."

Chad stared at him.

Then Richey stepped up onto the bench, towering above the lockers and players alike.

"I'm saying this to *all of you*," he called. "We can't go into this fractured. If we fight each other here, we *lose* out there. Jimmy's injury sucks. But this is still our team. This is still our season."

Heads nodded. Whispers died. Players turned toward him.

"I'm not perfect. But I'll give you every ounce of what I have. And if we all do the same? We don't just win — we dominate."

Silence followed. Tense. Charged.

Then Chad stepped forward. His brow furrowed. His jaw tight.

"So help me God, Richey... if we lose—"

"You can't think like that," Richey interrupted. "*I'm* not thinking like that."

Chad exhaled slowly. Something changed in his face.

Chad studied Richey for a long moment, conflict evident in his expression. Finally, he spoke, voice lower than before.

'My cousin was quarterback at Westlake last year. Tore his ACL mid-season. Nobody stepped up. Team fell apart.' He looked Richey in the eye. 'I don't want that happening here.

He nodded.

One sharp nod.

Then another.

"You screw up," he said quietly, "I'm still gonna flatten you in practice."

"I'd expect nothing less," Richey replied.

A grin passed between them — not friendly, but respectful.

Then, like thunder, Coach Kenneck's voice rang out from the hallway.

"C'MON LADIES! YOU PLAN TO WIN FROM THE LOCKER ROOM?"

The room jolted back to life. Shoulder pads clicked into place. Helmets snapped shut. Cleats clattered on tile.

Richey stayed back a moment, finishing his gear ritual. Right cleat, then left. Gloves laced and tucked. Towel looped through the waistband. Helmet cradled under his arm.

Coach Kenneck stepped inside and caught the tail end of the action.

"You rally 'em?" he asked, eyeing the still-buzzing room.

"I guess I did," Richey said, voice calm.

Coach gave a half-grin. "Then get your ass out there and lead, son."

"Yes sir."

Richey jogged to the door, paused at the threshold, and looked out onto the field. The sunlight was orange now, casting long shadows on the turf.

He stepped out.

And it began.

Practice Under the Sun

The stadium lights flickered on, buzzing faintly as they bathed the field in a soft golden haze. The sun hadn't set yet, but twilight was creeping in. The shadows were long, the air thick with moisture. The turf still held the day's heat, radiating it upward in gentle waves. Richey stepped onto it like a soldier onto a battlefield.

The rest of the team was already lined up, helmets glinting, bodies moving in drills — linemen on sleds, receivers running routes, backs working cuts. The rhythm of practice had begun. Whistles blew sharp and staccato, punctuating the air like gunfire.

Richey jogged toward the quarterbacks' corner. His cleats dug into the field with every stride, each step another beat in the drumline of his resolve. Coach Wilkes was waiting with the clipboard, tossing the ball hand to hand like he was warming it up.

"Glad you decided to show up," he said without looking up.

"Wouldn't miss it," Richey replied, reaching out and catching the ball in one fluid motion.

Wilkes finally looked up. "Today's no ordinary practice."

"I know."

"We've got recruiters in the stands. One from UT. One from Rice. Maybe a scout from Arizona. Don't look. Don't showboat. Just lead."

"I got it, Coach."

"Start with warm-up tosses. Then, two-minute drills. No dead reps."

"Yes, sir."

Richey dropped back and fired the first pass to his receiver. It sailed clean and crisp, spiraling across the field with textbook velocity. Another. Then another. Muscle memory took over — hips turning, shoulders locked, feet aligned. He didn't even think. He *knew*.

As the drills continued, something shifted. Players were sharper. The tempo was faster. There was urgency in every step, every call, every snap.

The offensive line — led by Chad — responded to Richey's commands with force and precision. They set the pocket like a wall. Even Chad's jabs turned to muttered grunts of encouragement.

"Let's go, Broke!"

"Nice ball, QB!"

The chemistry was forming — not perfect yet, but real. Richey could feel it.

Then came the two-minute drill.

Coach Kenneck blew the whistle and barked out the scenario:

"Ball on the 40. Down by four. No timeouts. 1:58 on the clock. GO!"

The entire team scrambled into place. Richey lined up under center, Chad snapping into his stance with a thud.

"Blue 42! Blue 42! Set!"

The ball hit his hands like a jolt. He dropped back. Pocket-held. He scanned — left, right, middle.

Receiver. Slant. Hit him in stride.

First down.

Again. No huddle.

"Trips right. Z jet motion. 38 sweep fake — flood right!"

Snap. Fake. Rollout. Find the tight end on the drag. Connect.

Tick, tick, tick.

Each snap built momentum. Each play pulled the team into a singular rhythm — one organism working together. The sideline was buzzing now. Defensive players started hooting.

Coaches shouted time.

Thirty seconds.

Twenty.

Red zone.

"Trips bunch left. Single back. Alert the fade!"

Richey took the snap, looked right, pumped — and fired left. The receiver leapt and came down in the corner of the end zone.

Touchdown.

The field exploded in shouts.

"WHOOOO!"

"Let's go!"

Even the defense clapped.

Richey walked off, chest rising with every breath. Sweat beaded on his brow. His heart thundered — but not from fear.

This was something else.

Confidence.

Belonging.

He looked to the bleachers. Three men in polo shirts stood near the press box, clipboards in hand. They had noticed.

Coach Kenneck pulled him aside.

"You lit that drill on fire."

Richey grinned. "Felt good."

"You're gonna start next Saturday," Kenneck said. "Official."

Richey swallowed hard. "Thank you, Coach."

Coach slapped his shoulder pad. "Earn it."

The team gathered for final stretches, the sky now purple with dusk. Practice wound down, but the energy lingered. Richey found himself laughing with a backup receiver. Chad even gave him a quick chest bump, almost jokingly.

As he peeled off his helmet, Richey turned toward the far end of the field, taking a moment alone.

He stood still.

Sweaty. Breathless. Alive.

His eyes scanned the field — the place that could change his life.

This wasn't just football.

This was freedom.

As they walked off the field, Chad fell into step beside Richey. They didn't speak at first, just walked side by side, helmets under their arms.

It was strange walking alongside someone who'd been nothing but hostile for years, but something had shifted during practice—a reluctant respect forming between them.

'That was decent,' Chad finally said. 'Better than I expected.' Richey nodded, keeping his expression neutral. He knew better than to seem too eager for Chad's approval.

'My cousin—the one who got injured last year—he never played again,' Chad continued. 'Said the worst part wasn't the injury. It was watching from the sidelines, knowing his backup wasn't even trying.'

'I'm trying,' Richey said. 'Yeah,' Chad agreed, surprising them both. 'I can see that.'

Before they reached the locker room, Chad added, 'My uncle's coming to the game. He's got connections at Rice. I'll make sure he watches you too.'

Party Detours

The car ride was quiet. The golden haze of late afternoon poured through the windshield, stretching shadows across the pavement like ribbons unraveling in slow motion. Mariana sat in the passenger seat, hair still damp from the pool, a light sheen of chlorine lingering on her skin. Her duffel bag lay at her feet, heavy with wet towels and yesterday's adrenaline.

Jackie's pop playlist buzzed gently through the speakers — catchy, energetic, but distant. Neither of them spoke at first.

Mariana's gaze drifted out the window. The city blurred past in sunlit fragments — trees, fences, fast food signs. But she wasn't seeing any of it. Her body hummed from the meet, heart still catching up to the rush she'd just lived through. The sound of the whistle, the explosive dive, the stillness before the splash — it replayed in slow loops in her head.

"You were *insane* today," Jackie finally said, eyes on the road. "I swear, I thought you were gonna shatter the pool tiles."

Mariana smiled faintly. "It felt good. Like... I wasn't even trying. My body just knew what to do."

"Coach Riley said that turn was surgical," Jackie added. "My cousin, the one who plays soccer at U of H? He was in the stands. He literally asked if you were Olympic-track."

Mariana laughed softly. "Let's not get carried away."

"No, seriously, people were talking about you. You're not just our girl Mariana anymore. You're *that girl* now."

Mariana leaned her head against the window. "It's weird. I thought I'd feel more... something. Proud, maybe. But all I feel is tired. Like all the work — the early mornings, the pressure — it's finally starting to catch up."

Jackie gave her a quick glance. "That's why tonight isn't just a sleepover. Tonight is *therapy*."

Mariana lifted her head. "Jackie..."

"I know, I know. You told your mom it was just us. And technically, it still is — just with some... musical guests."

They pulled into Jackie's driveway — an angular modern house with a clean stone facade and the kind of plants that never needed watering. Jackie killed the engine and turned to face her.

"Breathe later," she said. "Tonight, we celebrate."

Inside, the house was still. Too clean. Too quiet. No jackets on hooks, no clinking of dishes — just that sense of polished, temporary vacancy. Jackie's parents were definitely still in Boston. The entire house felt like it was holding its breath.

Jackie made a beeline for the kitchen, where several bottles stood arranged on the counter like soldiers. She grabbed a red cup and mixed something pink and strong-smelling.

"Want one?" she offered, already taking a long swig.

"Maybe later," Mariana said, watching with slight concern as Jackie grimaced and took another gulp. "You might want to pace yourself. It's still early."

Jackie waved her hand dismissively. "Please. I've been waiting for this night forever. Besides," she grinned, "someone has to get this party started." She refilled her cup, sloshing liquid over the rim, before heading upstairs. "Come on! Let's get ready!"

Mariana dropped her bag by the door. Her body was moving automatically now — up the stairs, into Jackie's room — like she was walking into a dream that was half-light, half-trouble.

As they climbed the stairs, Jackie confided in a half-whisper, 'Ryan was supposed to come tonight. We've been texting all week.' Her expression darkened. 'But now I hear he might bring Melissa instead. After he totally led me on.'

Jackie's room was its own world: vanity lights glowing like stage lights, stacks of clothes erupting from drawers, body spray misting the air like incense. A hair straightener hissed on the counter, already prepped for action.

"I'm so sick of this," Jackie continued, as she sat heavily on the bed. "Every time I like a guy, something goes wrong. Either they ghost me, or they're just using me to make someone else jealous, or..." She took another long sip from her cup.

Mariana had seen this pattern before. Since freshman year, Jackie had cycled through crushes and brief relationships that always ended dramatically. None lasted more than a few weeks.

"You know what my mom said when I told her about Ryan last week?" Jackie's voice hardened. "She said, 'That's nice, honey' and kept packing. Didn't even look up from her suitcase."

She stood abruptly, moving to the vanity mirror to check her makeup. "They've missed three of my birthdays because of 'unavoidable business trips.' Dad sent a diamond bracelet last year instead of showing up." She laughed, but it sounded hollow. "At least they left me the house this weekend. That's something, right?"

Mariana watched her friend with growing concern. Behind Jackie's party-girl persona was someone desperately seeking attention and validation—from boys, from peers, from parents who were physically and emotionally absent.

"Tonight is going to be different," Jackie declared, her mood shifting again as she returned to the closet. "I'm going to have fun, I'm going to forget about Ryan, and I'm going to make sure everyone remembers this party."

Mariana sat on the edge of the bed while Jackie rummaged through her closet.

"So," Jackie said changing the subject, tossing a lacy black top aside, "how's it feel being a legend?"

Mariana smirked as she thought about how different her parents where. "Like I might actually have a future. Maybe scholarships. Maybe... options."

"You're not maybe," Jackie said, turning with a grin. "You *are* the future. Mariana, NCAA heart-breaker, future Olympic bronze medalist — or gold, but I'm trying to be humble." She paused, then added with enthusiasm, 'And the birthday girl! Sweet sixteen and already breaking records. This party is totally your belated celebration.'"

Mariana's smile softened. "I just want my parents to know it was worth it. All the driving, the money, the sacrifices."

"They do," Jackie said. "Trust me. Your mom was watching like her whole soul was in that pool with you."

That hit Mariana unexpectedly hard.

"She waved," she said quietly. "She *knew*. She could tell I was spiraling, and she grounded me. Like she always does."

Jackie sat beside her, their shoulders nearly touching. "Your mom's a superhero. But tonight? You're not someone's daughter. You're not Captain Mariana. You're just a girl who swam her heart out and deserves to *breathe*."

Mariana looked down at her phone. "I still told her I'd call before bed. She thinks I'll be at your house, asleep by ten."

Jackie hesitated — then dropped her voice. "You *will* be here. It's just... a slight detour on the road to slumber."

Mariana raised an eyebrow. "Jackie, what kind of detour?"

Jackie's eyes twinkled mischievously. "The *fun* kind. Daniel's cousin already dropped off drinks. People are coming. Low-key at first — music, snacks, maybe karaoke. But later? I mean... Richey might show."

Mariana's head snapped up. "Richey?"

Jackie grinned. "Girl, don't act like you haven't noticed. He watches you. *Everyone* knows it."

Mariana felt the heat rise in her cheeks. "No, he doesn't."

"He does. He talks to Daniel about you. You should've seen the way he looked at you in class. Like... you were sunlight."

Mariana groaned. "Stop."

Jackie tossed a silky off-the-shoulder top at her. "Try that. It says: national champion *and* cool enough to have fun."

Mariana held it in her lap, fingers brushing the smooth fabric. "I don't know, Jackie. I've been so careful for so long. My parents — especially my mom — they've made everything about protecting us. And I *get* it. But sometimes it feels like I'm not even living."

Jackie didn't speak right away. Then, softly: "Then live tonight. Just a little. You don't have to drink. You don't have to make out with anyone. You don't even have to stay past midnight. But come downstairs. Laugh too loud. Dance badly. Feel something that isn't pressure."

Mariana looked out the window, the sun now dipping into twilight. The sky was painted in pinks and purples — a quiet, strange beauty.

She thought about the sacrifices. The mornings. The weight.

And the way it felt when Richey smiled at her — shy, a little crooked, like he wasn't used to being seen.

"What if I mess up?" she whispered.

"Then you do," Jackie said. "And maybe it teaches you something. Or maybe it becomes a story. Or maybe — just maybe — it becomes a moment you never forget."

Mariana stood slowly, holding the top in both hands.

"One party," she said. "One night."

Jackie shrieked and spun. "YES. Okay, okay — we need glitter. Or maybe dewy. What do you think: chill goddess or party star?"

They spent the next half hour tearing through outfits, experimenting with lip gloss and highlighter, switching playlists on and off. It was messy and chaotic and perfect. Mariana caught her reflection in the mirror — and for the first time, she didn't see the captain or the immigrant daughter. She just saw herself.

Later, as they headed downstairs, the first knock came at the door. Laughter bubbled through the air. Music turned up.

Mariana hesitated, one hand still on the stair railing.

"Still time to back out," Jackie teased behind her.

Mariana smiled. "Not a chance."

And down they went.

Into the night.

The party filled the house quickly, music throbbing through speakers, voices rising to compete with the bass. Mariana lost track of Jackie for a while, only spotting her periodically through the crowd— each time with a different drink, each time louder, her gestures becoming more exaggerated.

"Have you seen Chelsea?" Jackie suddenly appeared at Mariana's side, her words slightly slurred. "She brought her cousin who goes to Westfield. Who invites Westfield people to my party?"

"I don't think—" Mariana started.

"Oh my God, is that Ryan with Melissa?" Jackie's mood shifted instantly, her eyes narrowing. "She knows I like him." Without waiting for a response, she pushed her way through the crowd, drink sloshing over the sides of her cup.

Throughout the next hour, Mariana caught glimpses of Jackie— arguing intensely with a girl in the kitchen, crying in a corner with mascara streaming down her face, then laughing hysterically minutes later with a different group. Each time their eyes met across the room, Jackie would wave wildly or blow exaggerated kisses, but there was something increasingly unstable in her demeanor that made Mariana uneasy.

Shadows at Home

The garage door creaked open like a tired sigh, dragging across rusted hinges that had been squealing for years. Richey wheeled his bike in and parked it against the wall, kicking aside a crushed soda can. It rattled across the concrete and pinged off the base of the old washing machine, leaving a black scuff mark against the chipped white paint.

The air was heavy — a cocktail of stale smoke, grease, and that quiet undercurrent of something metallic and sour. The kind of smell you didn't notice after a while, because it was part of the wallpaper of your life.

Richey paused for a moment, fingers still on his handlebars. The house was too quiet — the kind of quiet that didn't mean peace. It meant someone was brooding.

He stepped inside. The kitchen light above flickered — that buzz and dim, buzz and brighten — like it couldn't decide if it wanted to be alive. The television was on in the living room, volume muted, showing a game show from decades past. Something Richey's dad liked — or maybe just left on because silence made him more uncomfortable than reruns.

His father was there in the recliner, like always. Cigarette dangling from one hand, the ashtray next to him overflowing — a tiny, smoldering graveyard.

"You're late," came the voice. Gravel-rough. Soured by drink.

"I had practice," Richey said, setting his bag down by the couch. "Coach kept us late. Looks like I'll be starting next Saturday."

There was a pause — just long enough to sting — and then the sound of the recliner creaking as his father leaned back and took a drag.

"Practice," he scoffed. "You still on that bullshit?"

Richey said nothing. He moved to the kitchen, opened the fridge, and grabbed a water bottle. The plastic was slick in his hand. He could feel the heat rising in the back of his neck already.

His father didn't stop.

"You could be working. Earning. But nah, you wanna chase that quarterback fantasy like it's gonna fix anything."

"I'm doing what I can," Richey muttered, turning around. "I'm doing something."

"Yeah?" His dad finally looked at him. His eyes were bloodshot, red rims wrapped in yellow haze. "You gonna throw a football at the rent next month? Gonna spiral one into the damn fridge when it breaks again?"

Richey swallowed hard. His stomach burned. He wanted to tell him. About the scouts. The reps. The way the whole team had rallied behind him, about Coach Kenneck's nod of respect. About *Chad*, of all people, giving him props. That he'd thrown a perfect two-minute drill.

But he already knew.

It wouldn't matter.

None of it ever did here.

"Not tonight," Richey said. "Please."

His father shook his head, already turning away again. "One day the world's gonna hit you like a brick, boy. And I hope you ain't too soft to take it."

That one hit harder than the others. It wasn't just the insult. It was the *finality* in his tone, like he'd already given up on the idea that Richey could ever be more than the walls around them.

Richey stood there for a long moment, water in hand, heart

thudding slow and sharp. Then he turned and walked up the stairs. Each step creaked, like the house itself wanted to drag him back down.

His room was dark. The old fan spun lazily overhead, pushing warm air in circles. He flopped onto his bed and stared at the ceiling. The blades blurred together, dust clinging to the edges like dead dreams.

He didn't even feel mad. Just... *exhausted.*

I don't belong here.

He thought about college. Any college. A dorm room. A locked door. Silence he chose. A bed that didn't remind him of nights he'd cried as a kid, hiding the bruises under his sheets.

A knock.

Not at the door — at the window.

Tap. Tap. Tap.

Richey sat up fast and peered through the blinds. Daniel.

He slid the window up. Cool air swept in.

"Yo," Daniel whispered. "You alive?"

"Barely."

Daniel grinned. "C'mon. Let's go—Jackie's party's starting. Whole school's coming. You need to *celebrate.*"

Richey hesitated. "Coach wants me sharp. I probably shouldn't."

"Dude," Daniel said, pulling himself halfway through the frame. "You *saved* practice today. You lit it up. You earned this."

Richey sat on the windowsill. He could still hear the muffled sound of the TV downstairs—the empty clink of a bottle hitting wood.

He nodded. "Gimme five."

They snuck around to Daniel's house, just three blocks over. His older brother wasn't home, which meant open closet access. Daniel's brother had always been the stylish one — sharp jackets, dark jeans, cologne that cost more than a month of gas money.

Daniel tossed him a black button-down and a pair of slim, dark jeans. "Put these on. You look like someone whose curfew is 'never have fun.'"

Richey changed slowly. His thoughts were still at home. Still in that recliner. Still hearing that voice.

"You ever think," Richey asked as he buttoned the shirt, "that we're all just trying to prove something to people who'll never care?"

Daniel turned, caught off guard.

Richey shrugged. "My dad doesn't care if I go pro. Doesn't care if I rot in this town. So, who am I doing this for?"

Daniel paused. "For you."

"That's the thing," Richey said. "I don't even know if I believe in me half the time."

Daniel walked over, dead serious for once. "I do. So does Coach. And Chad, weirdly. And maybe... Mariana."

Richey blinked. "What?"

"She might be at the party."

That froze him.

"She even *knows* who I am?"

"Bro," Daniel laughed. "She sits in front of you. She talks to you. She *definitely* notices. I think she likes the quiet ones."

Richey looked in the mirror. For once, he didn't hate the reflection.

"I don't know what to do. What to say."

"Just show up. That's step one."

As they walked out to Daniel's car, the cool night air hit them — sharp, promising, electric. The world smelled different at night. Like anything could happen. Like freedom.

Richey patted his pocket, feeling the bulge of his old flip phone. While everyone else pulled out iPhones to check social media on the way, he'd be sitting in silence. But tonight, it didn't bother him as much. The flip phone was reliable. Simple. Functional. Just like he wanted to be.

They pulled out of the driveway. Music playing low. The party just a few streets away.

Richey looked out the window, trying not to over-think everything. But he knew what was waiting at home if he stayed. The ashtray. The scowl. The bitterness. The weight.

And what waited ahead?

He didn't know.

But maybe — just maybe — for one night, he could try something else.

He could forget the yelling.

Forget the silence.

Forget the history carved into every crack of that damn recliner.

And maybe — if the stars aligned — he could remember what it felt like to be *wanted*.

To be *seen*.

To be *enough*.

First Connection

Laughter pulsed from the backyard like a heartbeat. Music thumped through the walls, lights flashing behind drawn curtains. Cars lined both sides of the street, some double-parked, their hoods still warm. The porch was lit with string lights — casual, almost too charming for what was clearly becoming the party of the semester.

Richey stepped out of Daniel's car, the sound of bass and chatter already settling into his chest. His heart was racing, though he tried not to show it. The borrowed clothes felt foreign against his skin – nicer than anything hanging in his own closet, a costume for a role he wasn't sure he could play.

"You ready for this?" Daniel asked, shutting the door with a confidence Richey wished he could bottle and drink.

"No," Richey said honestly, tugging at the collar of his borrowed shirt. "But I'm here."

Daniel smirked. "That's 90% of the battle."

They walked up the path. Richey felt the shift immediately — the eyes, the energy, the sense that he was stepping onto a different stage now. Someone from the porch called his name. Another clapped him on the back.

QB1.

He hated that nickname. But tonight, he wore it like armor, protection against the vulnerability of being here – of wanting something, someone, he'd watched from a distance for too long.

"Easy, man," Daniel murmured, sensing his tension. "Just another party."

But it wasn't. Not for Richey. This was uncharted territory, a world where people like him – second-string quarterbacks with alcoholic fathers and secondhand clothes – didn't typically venture by choice. A world where girls like Mariana Garcia existed, effortlessly beautiful and impossibly out of reach.

Until maybe tonight.

Mariana stood near the kitchen, cup in hand, untouched. She wasn't sure what was in it. Stephanie had handed it to her before disappearing into a crowd of soccer players. The liquid was pink, vaguely tropical, and definitely spiked with something that smelled like her father's whiskey cabinet on holidays.

The room was warm, too loud, too bright. Laughter spilled from every corner. Someone had already spilled something sticky on the tile, and Jackie — still barefoot — danced around it like it was a lava pit, her movements becoming less coordinated with each drink.

Mariana had changed twice. She'd finally settled on black jeans and the off-the-shoulder top Jackie insisted made her look like a Netflix protagonist. Her hair was curled slightly at the ends, her lip gloss subtle, her eyes lined in a way that made them seem deeper, darker.

Still, she didn't feel like herself.

She was used to chlorine. Schedules. Control. Early mornings and disciplined routines that left no room for this kind of spontaneity.

This — this chaos — was foreign. Exhilarating and terrifying in equal measure.

She checked her phone again, guilt flickering as she dismissed another text from her mother. *Just checking in, mija. Call before bed.* She would. But not yet. Not before she had something – anything – to make this risk worthwhile.

"Stop scanning the room like a lifeguard," Jackie whispered, appearing beside her. "You're allowed to relax."

"I am relaxed," Mariana lied, her shoulders betraying her as they tensed even further.

"You look like you're preparing for a hostage negotiation." Jackie grinned, swaying slightly as she bumped Mariana's hip with her own. "Loosen up. Have fun. Maybe even talk to someone who isn't on the swim team."

Before Mariana could respond, the front door opened — and time slowed.

Richey stepped in.

She noticed him before anyone else did, her swimmer's vision catching the movement across the crowded room with perfect clarity.

The way his shoulders pulled slightly tighter when people greeted him. The way his hand hovered, unsure, before slipping into his pocket. His hair was slightly messy, like he'd run his hand through it five too many times. He was wearing a black button-down, sleeves rolled, collar just slightly askew.

He looked uncomfortable.

And impossibly magnetic.

She turned away fast.

Too fast.

Jackie raised an eyebrow. "Oh no. You're blushing."

"I am not," Mariana said, already sipping the mystery drink to hide her face. The sweetness barely masked the burn of alcohol, and she tried not to wince.

"You like him," Jackie sang, grinning. "You're gonna marry him and have little athlete babies."

"Stop," Mariana hissed, heat climbing her neck. "He doesn't even know I exist."

"You sit in front of him. You gave him a pen. You said his name. That's practically intimacy in teenage language."

Mariana groaned, hoping the dim lighting concealed how accurately Jackie had read her. For months, she'd been hyperaware of Richey

Vance's presence behind her in class – the quiet way he'd answer questions when called upon, the faint scratch of his pencil, the way the air seemed to shift when he'd lean forward.

But that was different. That was school. This was... real life. With no assigned seating or bell schedule to dictate their interaction.

Across the room, Jackie's friend Melissa was watching them, her eyes narrowed despite her smile. She raised her cup in a mock toast when she caught Mariana looking, then whispered something to the girl beside her, both of them giggling while continuing to stare. Mariana shifted uncomfortably, turning her back to give herself some privacy.

Just then, Richey's eyes found her.

And held.

Their first real gaze. Not stolen glances. Not classroom flickers.

Locked.

He didn't smile. He just looked, with an intensity that made her forget the music, the party, her own name. As if he was searching for something in her face that he'd been looking for his entire life.

And she didn't look away.

Couldn't.

———

Daniel elbowed him. "Dude."

"What?" Richey answered, though he hadn't stopped looking at Mariana. She wore her hair down tonight, different from the tight ponytail she wore for swimming. It framed her face in soft waves, making her look both familiar and like someone he'd never seen before.

"She's right there. This is your movie moment. Don't screw it up."

"I don't know what to say." Panic flickered through him, his carefully rehearsed greetings evaporating like mist.

"Start with 'Hi.' Work your way up to full sentences." Daniel shoved him lightly. "Go. Before I start telling everyone about that time in fifth grade when you—"

"I'm going," Richey said quickly, cutting him off.

He took a breath, steadying himself. In his mind, he could hear his father's voice, the familiar cruel dismissal: *What makes you think a girl like that would want anything to do with you?* He pushed it away. Not tonight. Tonight was about possibilities.

And walked.

Every step felt significant, like crossing an invisible boundary that had existed between them for years. Between who they were supposed to be and who they might become together.

———

Mariana felt it before she saw it — that quiet shift in energy when someone's moving toward you, like gravity bending slightly. Her pulse quickened, and she set her cup down on a nearby table, suddenly wanting clear hands, clear thoughts.

He stopped a foot away, close enough that she could smell the faint trace of mint on his breath, see the way his borrowed shirt pulled slightly across his shoulders.

"Hey," he said, voice quieter than she expected. Almost reverent, like a prayer in a silent church.

"Hi," she replied, surprised at the steadiness of her own voice.

Silence.

Not awkward, exactly. But weighted with everything unsaid. The acknowledgment that this wasn't an accident or coincidence – they had both chosen to be here, in this exact spot, at this exact moment.

The music changed — something softer, more rhythmic. People swayed nearby, but it all felt distant, as if the world had contracted to just this small pocket of space they inhabited together.

"I didn't think you'd come," she said, because it was true. Girls like her didn't expect boys like him to show up at parties like this. Not because he wasn't welcome, but because she'd always sensed that same wariness in him that she felt – the careful distance kept from chaos, from unpredictability.

"Me neither," he admitted, and the honesty in those two words created a bridge between them.

Richey remembered seeing her last month in the school library, surrounded by textbooks but staring out the window, something wistful in her expression that had made him wonder what she was thinking about. He'd wanted to ask then, but the moment had passed, as all their moments seemed to do.

Until now.

"You clean up nice," she offered, gesturing vaguely at his outfit, then immediately feeling foolish for the generic compliment.

He looked down at himself, a self-deprecating smile tugging at his lips. "Credit goes to Daniel's closet."

She smiled, relaxing slightly. "It fits you."

"You too," he said, realizing the awkwardness of the phrase too late. "I mean—your outfit. It... suits you. In a good way. Not that you don't always—"

"You're spiraling," she observed, biting back a smile.

"I'm aware," he said, running a hand through his already-disheveled hair. "Public speaking isn't my strong suit."

She laughed, the sound warm and genuine. "It's kind of endearing."

The tension eased further, something more comfortable sliding into place between them.

He scratched the back of his neck. "I'm not really good at this."

"At what? Talking?"

"At... parties. Talking to girls. Being seen." The last word held a weight that hung in the air between them, a confession she hadn't expected.

Mariana tilted her head, studying him with new interest. "Well, you're doing fine so far."

"You think?"

She nodded. "Better than most." And it was true. Most boys approached her with rehearsed confidence, with lines and expectations. His honesty was refreshing, disarming in a way that made her want to reciprocate.

He looked at her for a long beat, as if gathering courage. "You were incredible today."

Mariana blinked, thrown by the change in subject. "You watched?"

"Yeah." A slight flush colored his cheeks. "Your last turn — the underwater one? It was like watching someone fly."

The compliment caught her off-guard, not just for its specificity but because it wasn't about how she looked or what she wore. It was about what she could do. What she had worked for.

Mariana felt something in her chest loosen. "Thank you."

"You ever think about going pro?"

She smiled, appreciating that he asked what she wanted, not what was expected. "I don't know. Some days I want that. Other days, I want to disappear for a year and sleep."

He chuckled, a warm sound that she felt rather than heard. "I feel that."

They stood in silence again, but it wasn't uncomfortable now. It felt... suspended. Like being underwater in that perfect moment between strokes, where the world goes quiet and time stretches like taffy.

The party continued around them, but they had created a small island of stillness in the chaos. Someone bumped into Richey from behind, pushing him slightly closer to her. He steadied himself, his hand briefly touching her arm, and the contact – though fleeting – left a warmth that lingered.

"So," she said, finding herself wanting to know more, to prolong this unexpected connection, "are you this intense with all your conversations?"

His eyes met hers, unwavering. "Only with people I actually want to talk to."

Her smile faltered, just slightly, caught off-guard by his sincerity. "Why me?"

The question hung between them, more vulnerable than she'd intended. But she wanted to know – needed to know – what had made him cross the room, what had made him notice her beyond their shared classes and stolen glances.

"Because you're not loud," Richey said after a moment, choosing his words carefully. "But you're... present. You make the room feel quieter. Like I can breathe."

Mariana didn't know what to say to that. The simple truth of it disarmed her completely.

So she said nothing.

Instead, she recognized the same sensation he described – the way the party's chaos seemed to recede when they spoke, the way his presence created a pocket of calm.

Then, softly: "Wanna go outside?"

He nodded, relief and anticipation mingling in his expression.

They slipped out through the sliding glass door, into the cooler night. The backyard was string-lit and half-full of people, but the far corner by the garden was empty, a forgotten space beyond the reach of music and voices.

They sat side by side on the grass, close enough that their shoulders almost touched. The night air was cool but not cold, carrying the scent of jasmine from somewhere nearby. Above them, stars punctured the darkness, impossibly bright against the Houston sky.

"Feels good to sit," she murmured, the tension of the evening finally easing from her shoulders. Here, away from watching eyes and expectations, she could finally breathe.

"I might just lie down and never get up," he said, leaning back on his elbows, his face tilted toward the sky.

She studied his profile in the dim light, noting the strong line of his jaw, the slight furrow between his brows that never quite disappeared. Even relaxed, he carried a watchfulness about him, as if waiting for something to go wrong.

She leaned back on her hands, mirroring his posture. "So what happens now?"

He looked at her, really looked, with a directness that would have been unnerving from anyone else. "I don't know. I never really thought I'd get here."

"Where's here?" she asked, genuinely curious about how he saw this moment, this connection that felt both fragile and significant.

"This," he said, gesturing vaguely between them. "Talking to you. Not feeling like I'm failing at every breath."

The admission struck her deeply – the idea that someone as talented and quietly compelling as Richey Vance could feel like he was constantly falling short. It resonated with her own carefully hidden fears, the pressure she carried beneath her achievements.

She looked at him — really looked. Beyond the borrowed clothes and quiet demeanor, beyond the label of "backup quarterback" or "that guy from English class." She saw someone fighting the same battles she was, just on different terrain.

"You're not failing," she said with quiet certainty, finding she meant it more than she'd expected to.

And for a moment, neither of them spoke.

Not because they didn't have anything to say.

But because the silence between them felt full.

Like the beginning of something neither had dared to hope for.

In the distance, the party continued – music pulsing, voices rising and falling, the world spinning on without them. But here, in this forgotten corner of Jackie's backyard, time seemed to pause, giving them space to exist outside of expectations and labels and predetermined paths.

Just two people, seeing each other clearly for the first time.

And finding something worth staying for.

Between Lines

The party had changed.

The lights were lower now, the music louder — vibrating through the floorboards, spilling into every hallway. Voices overlapped into a steady, drunken hum. Someone had cleared the coffee table and turned it into a makeshift dance floor. Empty cups and crushed soda cans lined the counters. The smell of too many perfumes, cologne, and sugary drinks lingered in the air like a fog.

Richey and Mariana reentered through the back patio door and stood in the living room's edge like visitors in a museum of barely-contained chaos.

The energy was different now — looser, messier.

"What did we just walk back into?" Mariana asked, raising her voice over the bassline.

"End-stage adolescence," Richey said, eyes scanning the room. "Or a deleted scene from *Euphoria*."

A guy stumbled by and nearly knocked into them, sloshing pink punch down his shirt. Mariana pulled Richey gently to the side, and the touch — even brief — left a warmth on both of their arms.

They retreated to a quieter corner of the room, tucked near the stairwell. Someone had dropped a hoodie there, and Richey offered it to her like it was a seat cushion.

She smiled and sat down, crossing her legs, her posture relaxed but her eyes still wide — observing everything.

"I don't do this," Mariana said after a moment. "Parties. Loud music. People spilling drinks. Lying to my mom. Especially not after big meets. Usually I'd be home resting, preparing for tomorrow's relays. Coach would kill me if he knew."

Richey leaned against the wall next to her, knees bent, looking out at the swirl of bodies. "Yeah, me neither."

She tilted her head. "Then why are you here?"

He hesitated. "Because for once, I didn't want to be *home*. And I didn't want to be invisible."

She looked at him carefully. "You're not invisible, Richey."

His eyes flicked to hers, then back to the crowd.

Why are you here?' he asked. 'If it's not usually your thing.'

'It's my birthday. Well, was. Thursday. Jackie insisted we celebrate.'"

Richey's attention trailed to the evolving party.

"My dad thinks football's a waste of time," he said softly. "That practice is just an excuse not to get a real job. That everything I'm doing is pointless. No matter what I do, it's not enough."

Mariana's expression softened. "I'm sorry."

"It's fine. I mean, it's not — but I've kind of... adapted to being disappointment adjacent."

She exhaled through her nose. "I get that more than you think. My parents — they love me, they do. But they carry so much of where they came from. Sometimes I feel like I'm stuck between their past and my future."

"Like you can't move without breaking something?"

"Yes," she said, surprised. "Exactly that."

They were quiet again. Not awkward — just still.

The music outside the moment blurred, muffled, irrelevant.

"I used to think," Mariana began, "that if I got straight A's, trained hard enough, followed the rules... I could buy their peace of mind. Like, if I was perfect, they'd never have to worry."

Richey nodded. "But then you realize they'll always worry."

"And you'll never be perfect."

They shared a look.

Then, laughter — not because anything was funny, but because it felt like a pressure valve finally released.

From the kitchen, someone shouted, and a loud *crash* followed — a bottle or maybe a blender. Jackie's voice rang out, half-laughing, half-scolding. The music surged louder. The room dimmed another notch as someone hit the lights, and now it was mostly just silhouettes moving to the beat, some locked together, others orbiting like planets.

"You wanna get out of here?" Richey asked suddenly.

Mariana blinked. "What?"

"I mean — not *leave* leave. Just... away from the noise. Upstairs, maybe. Somewhere where I can hear you think."

She gave him a mock-suspicious look. "Is this your version of a line?"

"No," he said quickly. "I swear. If I were making a move, it'd be smoother."

She grinned. "Good to know you're self-aware."

As they turned toward the stairs, Jackie materialized in front of them, swaying slightly. Her mascara had smudged beneath one eye, and her drink—at least her fourth or fifth—was dangerously close to spilling.

"Where are you two sneaking off to?" she asked, her voice overly sweet but with a sharp edge.

"Just somewhere quieter to talk," Mariana explained.

Jackie looked between them, her expression cycling rapidly between amusement and suspicion. "Upstairs is off-limits," she said firmly, then abruptly laughed. "Just kidding! Have fun, you crazy kids!" She stumbled slightly, catching herself on Mariana's arm. "But not too much fun, right? Because Mariana's a good girl. And good girls don't..."

"We're just talking, Jackie," Richey said quietly.

Jackie's smile remained fixed, but her eyes hardened. "Sure, sure. Just be careful with this one," she stage-whispered to Richey, loud enough for Mariana to hear. "She looks all innocent, but..." She trailed off with a theatrical wink.

"Maybe you should get some water," Mariana suggested gently.

"Maybe you should mind your own business," Jackie snapped, then immediately switched back to smiling. "Just being a good host! I'll check on you guys later." She spun away, immediately drawn into another conversation, though her eyes kept tracking them as they headed for the stairs.

Mariana felt a chill despite the crowded room's heat. There was something in Jackie's gaze that felt unpredictable.

They weaved past the crowd. The second floor was quieter, though not silent. A couple rooms had doors cracked with giggles and music leaking out, but the far guest bedroom — barely used, with a window view of the backyard — was still and dim.

Richey pushed the door open, waited for her to step in, then followed and shut it behind them.

The air in here was cooler. Quieter. A distant hum of the music pulsed through the walls like a heartbeat but didn't intrude.

They sat on the carpeted floor near the window, their shoulders close, the silence now richer — fuller, almost alive.

"Tell me something you don't tell anyone," Mariana said, her voice barely above a whisper.

Richey looked at her. "That's a big ask."

"Good," she replied. "I'm tired of small ones."

"I've never told anyone this stuff before," Richey admitted. "Not even Daniel, and he's known me since we were kids."

He took a breath.

"When I was eleven," he began slowly, "my dad forgot my birthday. I waited at the table for three hours. Finally, I lit one of my mom's old scented candles, stuck a toothpick in it like a candle, and sang to myself. Whispered it, really. Because it was worse to hear nothing."

Mariana said nothing. Just reached out and gently laced her fingers through his.

The touch stunned him. Not because of what it was — but because of what it wasn't.

It wasn't pity.

It was presence.

Mariana didn't look away.

"My parents..." she said after a moment, "they love so loudly it's hard to breathe. Their fear became my religion. Like I owed them proof that all their sacrifices meant something."

Richey squeezed her hand. "You are the proof."

The silence that followed was thick, humming with something unsaid. The music downstairs shifted again — slower now, deeper, almost cinematic.

"Why are we here?" Mariana asked suddenly, her voice almost a breath.

"At the party?"

"No. *Here*. Like this."

"I think," Richey said carefully, "that we've been orbiting each other for a while. And maybe tonight... we stopped spinning."

She looked at him.

Really looked.

Their knees were touching now. The air between them seemed thinner. Charged.

Outside the window, voices echoed from the yard. Someone screamed — laughter, then a splash. But none of it touched this moment.

Then something shifted.

A sudden *pop* from downstairs — maybe a champagne cork or a speaker glitch — startled Mariana. She instinctively moved closer, almost into his chest, her hand gripping his.

Richey didn't move.

She looked up at him.

He looked down at her.

Her breath caught.

She reached up, tentative at first, then certain — and kissed him.

Not hurried. Not hesitant. Just real. Soft and quiet and finally.

When they pulled apart, Richey's voice was low, almost disbelieving.

"That just happened."

Mariana smiled. "It did."

He leaned his forehead to hers.

"I've wanted to talk to you for so long," he said.

"You just did," she whispered.

And outside, the party roared on — louder, brighter, faster.

But here, in this quiet upstairs room, time had finally slowed.

The Misunderstanding

The room was quiet now. Not the false quiet of empty houses, but the **real quiet** that follows something meaningful.

Mariana's head rested gently on Richey's shoulder, her legs curled up against the bed's comforter. The soft glow of the backyard lights still flickered through the window, but they barely noticed. They weren't talking anymore — just *breathing*.

Richey had never felt this kind of stillness before. Not at home. Not at school. Not anywhere. There was no judgment, no need to impress. Just warmth. Her warmth. Her presence. The rhythm of her breath slowing as she drifted into sleep.

Her hand still rested lightly on his chest, and he was careful not to move too fast, afraid of waking her. She looked peaceful. Exhausted, yes — but peaceful. Her makeup had faded, and her curls had frizzed slightly at the edges, but to Richey, she looked like a secret he'd just learned to read.

She'd had a little to drink, but nothing wild. Just enough to loosen the tension in her shoulders, to laugh a little louder, to allow herself *this* — a night of not carrying the weight of being the captain, the daughter, the immigrant dream incarnate.

Richey glanced down at her.

"You okay?" he whispered.

No response — only the soft rise and fall of her chest.

She was out.

He stayed there a little longer, listening to the thump of the music downstairs grow faint again, then swell. The night wasn't over for most people. But up here, for them, it felt like it had just quietly concluded.

Finally, he moved carefully — lifting her hand off his chest, tucking the blanket over her shoulder. He stood, rolled his neck, ran a hand through his hair. His heart was still racing, not from desire, but from something purer.

Hope.

He needed a moment to breathe. To *look* at himself. He stepped into the hallway, gently pulling the door shut behind him, and made his way toward the upstairs bathroom.

The hallway was dim, lit only by the LED glow from someone's phone charger plugged into a socket. The bathroom mirror was a little cracked in one corner, toothpaste stains clinging to the sink edge. Richey splashed cold water on his face, then looked up at himself.

Same messy hair.

Same tired eyes.

But something felt different now.

He smiled. Just a little.

He adjusted his shirt, ran his hand over his jaw. For a second — just a second — he looked like a guy who belonged somewhere.

Then he opened the bathroom door.

And the night cracked open.

Downstairs, Jackie was searching the crowded rooms, her movements increasingly frantic. The buzz from earlier had soured into something darker, her emotions swinging wildly after seeing Ryan arrive with Melissa.

'Has anyone seen Mariana?' she demanded, grabbing a sophomore's arm. 'She disappeared with that football guy.'

'Upstairs, I think,' someone answered.

'Alone?' Jackie's eyes narrowed. Her protective instincts, already heightened by alcohol and jealousy, flared into something like suspicion. 'She doesn't even know him.'

Jackie took the stairs two at a time, her thoughts racing. First Ryan betrayed her, and now some random guy was taking advantage of her best friend at her party. Not tonight. Not in her house. Her heart pounded furiously, the room spinning slightly from alcohol and adrenaline. Memories flashed through her mind—Ryan choosing Melissa, her parents missing yet another birthday, Mariana always careful, always perfect.

Jackie felt a sudden fierce protectiveness. Mariana was vulnerable, and Jackie wasn't about to fail her tonight, not like everyone else had failed Jackie. Anger surged, sharpened by fear, clouding her judgment as she reached the hallway and saw Richey standing there, disheveled, nervous.

Jackie was standing, arms crossed, eyes scanning every room. Her makeup was smudged, her expression sharp with concern. She looked frantic, cornered.

"Jackie?" Richey said softly.

Her eyes locked onto him — shirt rumpled, hair tousled, skin flushed.

"What the hell are you doing up here?" she snapped.

Richey blinked. "I was just—"

"Where's Mariana?" Jackie barked, already moving past him.

"She's asleep. We were talking—"

"You were *in her room?*" Jackie's voice was rising. "With the door closed? She's drunk, Richey!"

"No — it wasn't like that. I swear. Nothing happened. She—she's just tired, that's all. We talked and—"

Jackie had already thrown the door open.

Inside: Mariana, still curled under the blanket, face half-turned to the side, cheeks flushed from sleep and drink.

To Jackie, it didn't look peaceful.

It looked wrong.

"WHAT THE HELL, RICHEY?"

The sound was sharp. Too loud.

Downstairs, someone heard it. Then someone else.

"What the hell did you DO?" Jackie shouted again, spinning around, her voice breaking with anger — and fear.

Richey raised both hands. "Nothing. I didn't touch her like that. I would never—"

"You're not supposed to be here," she spat. "She *trusted* you."

"I didn't do anything!"

"Then why are you SNEAKING out of the bathroom, looking like *that*?"

Voices were coming up the stairs now.

People were listening. Watching.

Daniel's voice was somewhere in the background — calling out, "What's going on?"

But it was too late.

Richey's chest was tightening. His ears were ringing.

Something ancient kicked in.

The *feeling* — that look on Jackie's face. That *rage* mixed with disbelief. That *accusation*.

It was the same expression his father had when Richey tried to explain anything — that grimace that said *you're lying, you're disgusting, you're a disappointment.*

Richey's breath shortened.

His hands shook.

"I swear to God, I didn't do anything," he whispered.

But Jackie wasn't listening anymore. She was too loud. Too afraid.

"You need to GET OUT!" Jackie screamed.

And Richey ran.

He didn't wait to explain. He didn't scan the room. He just bolted — down the stairs, two at a time, his breath ragged in his throat, heart thundering so loud it drowned out the party's chaos behind him.

Faces blurred past him. Voices shouted questions. Music stuttered, then died. But all Richey could hear was that one echo in his head:

She thinks I'm like him.

The front door slammed open as he threw himself through it, stumbling onto the porch. Cold air punched his lungs. He hit the yard at a sprint.

His chest was burning.

He had to get away. Far. Fast.

Anywhere but here.

Then he felt it — the jingle in his pocket.

His hand dove in instinctively.

Daniel's car keys.

His fingers closed around them like a lifeline.

Behind him, the front door flew open again.

"RICHEY!" Daniel's voice tore through the night. "Richey, WAIT!"

But Richey was already at the curb.

Already unlocking the car.

Already sliding into the driver's seat with trembling hands.

Daniel reached the front lawn just in time to see the headlights flare to life.

"Dude, what are you doing?!" he yelled, sprinting across the grass. "Just STOP — we can figure this out—!"

But the engine roared.

Tires shrieked against asphalt.

And just like that—

Richey peeled out into the night.

Gone.

The time on the dashboard read 10:42 PM. In less than twenty minutes, everything would change forever.

Vanishing down the street like a ghost chased by the only thing he'd ever truly feared:

Being seen the wrong way.

Calming Haze

The first thing Mariana noticed was the **throbbing** in her head.

Then the weight — a blanket, soft and warm, tucked around her body. The dim, unfamiliar light filtering through gauzy curtains. The distant *thump-thump* of bass, and voices echoing up from downstairs.

She blinked.

The room came into focus slowly — Jackie's guest bedroom, the one with the gray walls and dusty bookshelf, the one where she'd talked to Richey, where she'd laughed, where—

She sat up fast.

The blanket slipped off her shoulder.

Richey.

But he wasn't there.

She looked around. The room was empty. The air felt... *wrong.* Like someone had stormed through recently, rattled the molecules. Her heart started pounding, and she swung her legs off the side of the bed, feet touching the cold wood floor.

She stood slowly.

From the hallway, she heard raised voices. Then footsteps. *A lot* of them.

And then—Jackie.

Drunk.

Screaming.

"I TOLD YOU HE SHOULDN'T HAVE BEEN UP HERE!"

The words hit Mariana like cold water.

"What...?" she whispered, moving to the door just as it burst open.

Jackie stumbled in, hair wild, mascara streaked, a cup in one hand, the other pointing dramatically at the bed Mariana had just left.

"There!" she shouted to the growing crowd behind her. "She was PASSED OUT! And he was COMING OUT of the bathroom looking all disheveled like—like—"

She hiccupped.

"Jackie?" Mariana said. Mariana's stomach twisted sharply as reality crashed into her all at once. She looked from Jackie's wild eyes to the faces staring from the hallway—eyes wide, accusing, judging. Panic seized her chest, the familiar flutter escalating rapidly into something overwhelming.

"Wait—Jackie, stop. Where's Richey? Nothing happened!" Her voice shook with rising dread. Jackie was spiraling, too drunk to listen. Mariana pushed past her toward the door, her heart racing frantically. "Where is he?" she demanded, her voice louder now, desperate, trying to find someone—anyone—who understood.

"Jackie?" Mariana said, eyes wide. "What are you talking about?"

More people were crowding into the room now — half-drunk partygoers, classmates, strangers. Some holding phones. Some whispering.

"Wait, is that Mariana?"

"Did something happen?"

"Is this about Richey?"

Mariana's pulse skyrocketed. "Nothing happened. We talked. That's it. I—I fell asleep."

Jackie turned to her, furious and frazzled. "He was up here! Alone with you! And you were *out cold*! What was I supposed to think?!"

"Jackie," Mariana said, her voice cracking, "he didn't do anything."

"Then why did he RUN?"

"I—I don't know. I just—please, can everyone get out of the room?"

But no one moved.

More footsteps.

A girl in a red dress pushed through the crowd, snapping gum. "Jackie's losing it again."

"No, this is serious," someone else said. "She looks shaken."

"I'm *not* shaken!" Jackie barked. "I'm protecting my friend!"

"By yelling and accusing someone in front of half the school?" Mariana snapped, her voice finally rising. "By turning a quiet moment into a freaking *trial*?!"

That silenced the room.

For a second.

Then came the murmurs.

"I heard she kissed him."

"No, I heard *he* kissed *her*."

"Wait, they hooked up?"

Mariana stepped back, face pale, panic crawling up her spine. "Stop. Just—stop. You weren't there. None of you were. You're twisting everything!"

"Mariana," Jackie said, trying to soften, stepping forward, "you were *passed out*."

"I was asleep!" she cried. "From swimming. From *everything*! I had one drink. I was tired. We were talking, and I fell asleep. He didn't do anything."

"You sure?" someone asked from the back.

That's when the tears came.

Not out of sadness — but fury. Frustration. *Shame.*

Then—suddenly, *urgently*—Daniel pushed through the crowd, breathing hard, hair windblown.

"Where's Richey?" Mariana demanded the moment she saw him. "Where did he go?"

Daniel's eyes darted around the room, landing on her. "He's gone."

"What?" Jackie asked. "Gone where?"

Daniel's voice was breathless, stunned. "He took *my car*."

"What?!"

"I tried to stop him—he just ran out the door. Got in. Peeled out. I couldn't catch him."

The room fell completely silent.

Then Mariana, trembling, asked, "Why would he do that?"

Daniel stared at her for a long beat.

Then quietly: "He looked scared. Like something inside him snapped."

Jackie's hand went to her mouth.

The crowd around them shifted, uncertain now.

Someone whispered: "This is bad."

And it was.

Because no one knew where Richey was going.

No one knew what he was thinking.

And for the first time in her life, Mariana felt like her world had spun completely out of her control.

The Crash

The tires screamed against the road as Richey flew down the dark stretch of county highway, the streetlights flickering like dying stars above him. The dashboard glowed blue, bouncing shadows across his face. His hands were clenched tight around the steering wheel — white-knuckled, shaking.

The wind roared through the half-open window. Cold, sharp, like it wanted to slap the thoughts out of his head.

But they wouldn't stop.

They just kept coming.

She looked afraid.

Jackie was screaming.

Everyone saw.

They think I did something.

He gripped the wheel tighter.

The street blurred around him — houses melting into one another, headlights flashing by in the opposite lane like accusations. He was going too fast. The speedometer ticked past 55. Then 60. Then 65.

But he didn't care.

Every breath he took felt like it caught on barbed wire.

You were supposed to have a good night.

You were supposed to matter.

Now you're just another broken thing everyone wants to fix or throw away.

He saw her face again — Mariana — before he left. Still asleep, peaceful, warm. And then—

Jackie's voice, high and broken: "WHAT THE HELL DID YOU DO?"

Richey slammed his fist against the dashboard. The car swerved slightly. He corrected.

His eyes burned.

He hadn't cried since he was thirteen, but the tears were crawling up his throat now, hot and angry and ashamed. His whole life had felt like running from something — the screaming, the accusations, the silence — and tonight was supposed to be *different.*

It wasn't.

He flew through a yellow light, barely registering it.

A memory flashed across his mind, sudden and vivid—Mariana's face in the moonlight at Jackie's house, her eyes reflecting starlight as she looked at him. The quiet moment when she'd asked, "Why are we here?" and he'd felt seen for the first time in years.

"I think we've been orbiting each other for a while," he'd said. "And maybe tonight... we stopped spinning."

The warmth of her hand in his, her fingers gently laced through his own. Her quiet laugh when he'd said something honest. The way she'd looked at him—not at the second-string quarterback or Richey Broke, but at him.

The memory evaporated as quickly as it had come, leaving him cold and alone in the rushing car. One more connection he'd managed to destroy.

Daniels voice running after him came barreling back:

"Richey, WAIT!"

But he didn't.

Because when people yell, you don't explain.

You run.

You run because you know what yelling leads to. You know how it ends. And it's never with someone saying, *I believe you.*

He was seven again, standing in the kitchen, a broken glass at his feet. His father looming over him, beer breath and fury.

"What did you do, boy?" The alcohol-thickened voice. The raised hand.

"I'm sorry," he had whispered then. "It was an accident."

His father had laughed, a sound like gravel. "Sorry doesn't fix anything. Sorry is what weak people say." His eyes had narrowed, searching for something in Richey's face and not finding it. "You gonna cry now? Gonna run to your mama? Oh wait—she left. Wonder why that was."

That night, like so many others, he'd learned that explanations were useless. That "sorry" was just a target painted on your chest. That running—physically or into silence—was the only defense that worked.

Why would tonight be any different? Why would Jackie believe him? Why would anyone?

The road was darker now. Trees lined both sides, their shadows dancing under the headlights like ghosts. The music was off. The air felt thin.

His palms were sweating.

His foot pressed harder on the gas.

The clock on the dashboard glowed 11:01 PM. Nineteen minutes since he'd fled Jackie's house. Nineteen minutes that separated the life he knew from whatever came next.

You shouldn't be driving.

He hadn't drunk much. Just half a cup of that weird pink punch. Barely anything. He didn't even feel drunk.

But what if they breathalyzed him?

What if they *called the cops*?

What if—

He blew past a stop sign at an empty four-way intersection.

And didn't see the police cruiser until it was too late.

Blue and red lights exploded in his rear-view mirror.

His heart stopped.

For a full second, everything went quiet.

Then panic surged.

They're here for me.

They know.

They think I—

He punched the gas.

The engine growled, tires spinning as the car lurched forward.

The sirens blared behind him.

"Shit, shit, SHIT—"

He took a hard left at the next light, the tires shrieking. The car fishtailed, his shoulder slamming into the door. He corrected, barely, the road narrowing now into a two-lane stretch lined with chain link fences.

The sirens faded slightly behind him.

But he didn't stop.

Couldn't.

His breathing was ragged now. Short, shallow gulps. Like someone was pressing on his chest.

He felt like he was drowning.

Images fired through his brain like lightning strikes:

Mariana's smile.

His father's voice: *"One day the world's gonna hit you like a brick, boy."*

The screaming upstairs.

Daniel yelling his name.

The keys in his pocket.

The door slamming behind him.

His reflection in the mirror.

The words he didn't say.

The person he couldn't be.

A red light appeared ahead.

And he didn't see it.

Not in time.

Not through the blur.

Not through the tears.

He blew through it at 72 miles per hour.

And never saw the 18-wheeler barreling through the cross street until it was *right there*.

Time stretched impossibly thin. In that suspended moment before impact, a kaleidoscope of images flashed through Richey's mind:

His father, not drunk but clear-eyed, teaching him to throw a perfect spiral when he was nine—before the bitterness had hollowed him out completely.

Daniel's face the first time they won a game together, pure joy untainted by expectation or doubt.

Coach Kenneck nodding with something like respect after today's practice—the possibility of a future that might now never come.

His mother's last hug before she left for good, the scent of her perfume and the whispered "I'll call you" that became less frequent as years passed.

Mariana in class, the sun from the window turning her hair to amber, her pen moving across the page in that careful, deliberate way that matched everything else about her.

The gentle weight of her head on his shoulder as she slept, trusting him without knowing him. The kiss—hesitant then certain—that had made him feel, for just a moment, like maybe he was worth something after all.

All the things he might never have again. All the connections severed in one moment of panic. All the potential versions of himself— quarterback, college student, friend, son, someone worthy of love— slipping away as metal screamed against metal and time resumed its merciless forward rush.

The impact was instant.

Cataclysmic.

Metal screamed as it twisted.

Glass shattered like a shotgun blast.

Richey's body jerked violently sideways as the truck slammed into the passenger side. The car folded in on itself, spun mid-air, and crashed roof-first into a streetlight, sparks showering the road like fireworks.

The sound echoed through the night — a brutal *clang* followed by silence, then the faint hiss of steam and oil.

Inside, the world was sideways.

The driver's door had torn open, bent backward like paper. The windshield was a spiderweb of fractures. Smoke curled from the hood.

The radio flicked on randomly, playing a soft country ballad — some ironic song about finding peace on back roads.

Richey hung suspended by the seatbelt.

His chest heaved.

Blood from a gash above his eyebrow trickled down his face, mixing with sweat and tears.

He blinked once.

Twice.

Everything hurt.

But he was *alive*.

Somewhere in the distance, voices shouted.

Someone had seen.

A woman screamed. A man was calling 911.

Richey tried to move, but the pain shot through his ribs like a hot wire.

His eyes fluttered. He looked up — dazed — through the cracked windshield and saw the stars.

So clear. So bright.

So far away.

And in the broken glass of the mirror, his own reflection — battered, bloody, but unmistakably *him*.

Not the quarterback.

Not the disappointment.

Not the failure.

Just a boy who had finally crashed into the very thing he was running from.

The weight of being human.

And then, everything went black.

Saturday

The Call

The phone rang once.

Twice.

Three times.

The fourth ring cut through the house like a blade.

In the dead silence of the living room, it echoed — unnatural, urgent — weaving through cigarette smoke and stale beer like an intruder. The television was still on, casting pale blue light on the cluttered furniture. A copper pan infomercial droned in the background, trying to sell nonstick miracles to an audience long since passed out.

James Vance stirred on the couch like something rising from the grave. His shirt was half-unbuttoned, twisted sideways on his torso. One sock was gone. His belt had been loosened, the metal clasp digging into the beer gut he once called muscle. His hands still bore the ingrained grease stains from the machine shop where he'd worked the early shift.

The room smelled of unwashed sweat, smoke, and the unmistakable sharpness of cheap liquor drying in the carpet.

He groaned. Rubbed his face.

The phone rang again.

"Shit," he mumbled, dragging himself upright.

His vision swam. A half-empty bottle of whiskey teetered near the edge of the coffee table, surrounded by a perimeter of crumpled cans.

An ashtray overflowed beside it, dead cigarettes standing like headstones.

James blinked, trying to push back the static in his brain. He stood — slowly — every joint barking like a neglected dog. He shuffled toward the kitchen counter where the ancient landline still sat, its cord twisted like it had been choking for years.

He didn't check the caller ID. Nobody worth a damn called him anymore.

"Yeah," he rasped into the receiver, voice cracked, breath sour.

There was a pause. Not the pause of hesitation — the pause of *something bad* coming. He knew that tone. He'd heard it after his brother OD'd. After his mother fell.

"This is Nurse Calderon," came the voice, professional but warm. "From Memorial County Hospital. I'm calling regarding your son. Richey Vance."

His spine snapped straight.

"What about him?"

"There's been an accident. A few hours ago. He was brought in by ambulance after a vehicle collision."

Silence. His hand gripped the counter.

The nurse's voice softened.

"He's currently in ICU. Stable, but in critical condition."

The room went dead. The infomercial continued in the background, selling frying pans to ghosts.

James didn't breathe.

"What kind of accident?" he asked. His tone wasn't shocked. It was sharp. Like it was ready to punch something.

"Single-vehicle collision with a commercial truck. It appears he ran a red light at high speed. The car was totaled. He was found unconscious at the scene and transported here under trauma protocol. He's on assisted breathing."

James didn't realize he was shaking until his hand slipped on the edge of the counter.

"Was he—was he drunk?" The words tasted like poison.

"We won't know for certain until full tox results come back," Nurse Calderon replied. "But the doctors' priority is stabilizing him. He's sedated now. There was head trauma, chest impact. Internal injuries we're monitoring."

James's jaw clenched.

The nurse paused. "He's alone, Mr. Vance. We thought you should know."

He nodded, though no one could see him. His voice came out like ground-up gravel.

"I'll be there."

"ICU Ward 3, Room 214. Ask for me when you arrive."

The line clicked.

He stood for a full minute, phone still in his hand. The kitchen faded to a gray fog. The hum of the refrigerator. The hiss of the radiator. The weight of *everything he hadn't done right*.

Then he hung up.

He moved to the bathroom like a man underwater.

The mirror was a stranger.

His eyes were bloodshot, rimmed red with threadlike veins. The skin under them sagged like worn fabric. His beard was patchy, uneven. His jawline — once solid — now bloated, tired.

He turned on the faucet.

The water blasted ice-cold.

He splashed his face, gasped at the shock.

"Jesus, kid..." he muttered. "What the hell did you do?"

But the real question — the one he didn't want to say aloud — was: *What the hell did I do?*

He reached for the towel, wiped his face with the edge of his shirt instead. Then he went to the bedroom and opened his closet.

Everything smelled like cigarettes and sweat.

He grabbed the cleanest shirt he could find — stiff from drying on a chair. His jeans had a rip at the pocket and a faded ring of black from where oil had spilled last summer. He didn't care. He shoved his feet into his boots and glanced at the dresser.

The photo was still there.

Eighth grade. Richey in shoulder pads too big for him, holding a trophy nearly the size of his head. His smile crooked, nervous, proud.

James stared at it.

That was the last photo he had printed.

And now his son was in a hospital bed somewhere — silent, broken, maybe slipping through fingers James didn't know how to close.

He grabbed the keys and walked out the door.

––––––––––

The streets were empty. Sleepy. That blue-gray shade of early morning before sunrise bleeds the color back into the world. Streetlamps flickered. Porch lights glowed. Dew clung to every blade of grass like cold breath.

James drove in silence.

The truck hummed under him, the engine clicking with age. He didn't turn on the radio. Didn't touch his phone.

He just stared at the road, one hand on the wheel, the other fisted against his thigh.

Every block he passed felt like memory.

He was good at math when he was little.

Hated broccoli. Loved comic books. Always drew little lightning bolts on his notebooks.

First time he got in a fight — it was to protect some scrawny kid getting shoved in the hallway.

And what did I do?

Nothing.

Yell.

Drink.

Ignore.

The light ahead turned red.

James stopped.

And in the stillness, he saw it: the twisted wreckage. The mangled car frame. The red blinking lights. The smoke. The shape on the stretcher.

Alone.

He gripped the steering wheel until the leather creaked.

"Please," he whispered. "Please don't let this be the last thing."

The light turned green.

He pulled into the hospital parking lot ten minutes later.

It loomed above him — concrete, glass, fluorescent light. A building full of grief and machines and waiting.

He didn't get out right away.

He sat there.

Let the engine idle.

Let the panic come.

Then he opened the door.

And stepped into a morning he never expected to live.

Riding Home

The party was a mess.

Lights still flashed from cheap Bluetooth speakers. The music had gone hollow — just bass and distortion — but no one was dancing anymore. People hovered in the kitchen and hallways, whispering, processing, texting. The drama had eclipsed the party hours ago.

Mariana sat on the front steps, knees tucked to her chest, her sweater wrapped tightly around her shoulders. Her eyes were rimmed red, the mascara she'd so carefully applied hours ago now smudged at the corners.

Beside her, Daniel stood silently, rocking slightly on his heels. He hadn't said much since he came back from chasing Richey.

"He just... drove off?" Mariana asked for the third time.

Daniel nodded. "He was shaking. Looked like he didn't know where he was. And then—he just took off."

Mariana wiped her face, her breath hitching again.

"God, this wasn't supposed to happen. I just—"

She stopped herself. The words felt like glass in her throat.

"He's a good guy, Mariana," Daniel said, voice quiet. "Richey's been through more than he lets on. He's never had anyone actually... believe in him."

"I do," she said, her voice breaking. "That's the worst part. Nothing happened. And now he's out there thinking the worst of everything —

of himself."

Daniel hesitated. "I don't think he thinks the worst of you."

She gave him a sad smile. "I hope not. I don't even know where he is. What if he's hurt? What if something happened?"

Before Daniel could answer, headlights sliced through the darkness, sweeping across the lawn as her mother's SUV turned sharply into the driveway. Mariana's stomach dropped. She knew that driving—tight turns, deliberate movements. Her mother was furious.

"Dios mío," Mariana muttered under her breath, quickly wiping her face. "She's going to kill me."

The SUV jerked to a stop, the headlights still blazing, illuminating them like suspects in an interrogation. For a moment, nothing happened. Just the idling engine and Mariana's heart hammering in her chest.

Then the driver's door flew open. Gloria Garcia stepped out, her movements crisp and controlled—which, as Mariana knew, was far more dangerous than any outburst. Her mother's eyes swept across the scene like searchlights—taking in the house with its flashing lights, the clusters of teenagers trying to appear sober, the empty cups littering the lawn, and finally, landing on Mariana.

"Mariana Isabel Garcia," she called, her voice carrying across the yard with the precision of a thrown knife. Not shouting—Gloria García didn't need to shout to command attention.

Several nearby teenagers scattered instinctively.

Mariana stood, legs shaking slightly, Daniel rising beside her. She could see her mother cataloging everything—her smudged makeup, her rumpled clothes, her red-rimmed eyes. Nothing escaped that assessment.

"Mami, I can explain—" Mariana started.

Gloria held up one hand, stopping her daughter mid-sentence. She marched across the lawn, her gaze now fixed on the house behind them. "¿Dónde están los padres?" she demanded, her accent thickening with emotion. "Where are Jackie's parents?"

"They're not here," Daniel offered. "They never were."

Gloria's eyes snapped to him, narrowing dangerously. "And you are?"

"Daniel Patterson, ma'am," he said, straightening unconsciously under her scrutiny. "Richey's friend. I've been making sure Mariana's okay."

Something in Gloria's expression shifted—not softening, exactly, but recalculating. She took a deep breath, visibly reining in her anger.

"What happened here?" she asked, her voice tight with the effort of control. "And don't you dare lie to me, Mariana. Not now."

Mariana glanced at Daniel, then back at her mother. The weight of the night—the party, the kiss, Jackie's accusations, Richey's flight—crashed down on her again, and to her horror, fresh tears spilled down her cheeks.

"It's all messed up," she whispered. "Richey—he—" The words tangled in her throat.

Gloria's face transformed in an instant. The anger didn't disappear, but maternal concern pushed to the forefront as she reached for her daughter, one hand cupping Mariana's face.

"¿Estás lastimada? Did he hurt you?" The question came fierce and protective.

"No! No, Mami, it's nothing like that." Mariana shook her head vehemently. "Richey would never—he's good, he's kind. But Jackie thought—everyone thought—and now he's gone, he took Daniel's car and just drove off, and no one knows where he is."

Gloria's eyes darted between Mariana and Daniel, her expression calculating as she pieced the story together. "This boy... he ran away because of something that happened with you?"

"Because of something that didn't happen," Daniel clarified, stepping closer. "Jackie made assumptions. Started shouting accusations. Everyone heard. Richey panicked."

Gloria's jaw tightened. She looked back at the house, then at her daughter, who seemed smaller somehow, folded in on herself with worry and guilt.

"We need to go home," she said finally, her tone brooking no argument. "Now."

"But Richey—" Mariana protested.

"Is not your responsibility right now," Gloria cut her off. Her eyes softened fractionally. "Your father is worried sick. We deal with our family first."

She turned to Daniel, her demeanor shifting to something more businesslike. "You're Daniel?"

"Yes, ma'am."

"Thank you for staying with her. If you hear anything about this boy..." She hesitated, then reached into her purse and withdrew a business card. "Call our home. Any hour."

Daniel took the card, surprise flashing across his face at this unexpected gesture.

Mariana touched his arm. "Please... if you hear from Richey—he needs to know he didn't do anything wrong. I should've said something sooner. He just... ran."

Daniel looked at her for a long second. "We'll find him."

She nodded and let her mother guide her toward the car, Gloria's arm firm around her shoulders—half comfort, half restraint.

As they walked, Gloria leaned close to her daughter's ear. "You and I are going to have a very long talk, mijita," she said quietly. "About trust. About choices. About consequences."

"I know, Mami," Mariana whispered.

"But first," Gloria added, squeezing her shoulder, "we make sure you're okay. That's what matters most right now."

The unexpected gentleness in those words nearly broke Mariana again. She'd been prepared for rage, for disappointment—not for this complicated mixture of anger and love.

The car was silent for the first five minutes. Oppressively silent. Gloria drove with both hands gripping the wheel, her knuckles white, her posture rigid. The seatbelt clinked. The radio remained off. The only sound was the hum of tires against asphalt and the occasional turn signal clicking like a metronome for a conversation that wasn't happening.

Mariana stared out the window, her cheek pressed against the cold glass. Her thoughts looped like static.

She couldn't stop seeing his face.

The way his voice softened when he spoke about his dad.

The way he looked at her like she mattered.

The way his fingers trembled when she kissed him.

And then—

The yelling.

The accusations.

The panic in his eyes.

"Were you drinking?" her mother finally asked, her voice cutting through the silence like a blade.

Mariana closed her eyes. "A little. One cup. I swear."

"Was Jackie drinking?"

Mariana didn't answer.

"Answer me, Mariana," Gloria demanded, her voice rising slightly. "Was. Jackie. Drinking?"

"Yes," Mariana admitted quietly. "A lot. That's partly why she overreacted."

Gloria exhaled sharply through her nose. "Y los otros chicos? Were boys drinking too?"

"Some of them. Not Richey—not much, anyway."

Her mother's hands flexed on the steering wheel. "Dios mío, Mariana. Do you have any idea what could have happened? Teenage boys, alcohol, no adults?"

"It wasn't like that—"

"You don't know what it was like!" Gloria's composure cracked for a moment, her voice sharp with fear. "You are sixteen years old. You think you understand people? Situations? How quickly things can turn dangerous?"

She took a deep breath, visibly struggling to regain control. "You told me it was a sleepover. With Jackie's parents home."

Mariana's voice cracked. "I know."

"You lied to my face. To my face, Mariana."

There was a long pause. The kind that could break things.

"Was there a boy?" she asked more quietly. "This Richey. Were you with him... alone?"

Mariana looked down at her lap. Her hands were clenched in her sweater. "Yes."

Her mom didn't respond.

And that silence — that silence hurt more than any shouting.

"I didn't lie to you because I don't care," Mariana whispered. "I lied because I wanted to live. Just a little. You and Papi, you keep me in this perfect little box. Captain of the swim team. Perfect grades. Perfect daughter. Sometimes I can't breathe."

Gloria flinched as if she'd been slapped. For a moment, her carefully controlled expression crumbled, revealing a flash of raw hurt that made Mariana instantly regret her words.

"We came to this country with nothing," Gloria said after a long moment, her voice low and intense.

"Left everything behind. Family. Friends. Everything familiar. Do you know why?"

"For opportunities," Mariana recited, the familiar narrative suddenly feeling hollow.

"For you," Gloria corrected. "For you and Vanessa. So you wouldn't have to fight for every scrap the way your father and I did. So you could have choices we never had." She shook her head. "And now you throw it all away for what? A party? A boy you barely know?"

"I'm not throwing anything away," Mariana protested. "It was one night."

"One night can change everything, mijita," Gloria said, her voice softening slightly. "One choice. One moment."

Her mother kept her eyes on the road. "You're sixteen, Mariana. You don't get to control everything yet. That's not punishment. That's protection."

"I wasn't in danger."

"Then why are you crying?"

That caught her. Mariana looked away, biting her lip so hard she tasted blood.

"Because I hurt someone," she said. "And I didn't mean to. I cared about him. I still do."

Her mother's hands tightened slightly on the wheel. But her voice softened.

"Was it serious?"

Mariana shook her head, then nodded. "I don't know. But it felt... real. Like I wasn't pretending for once."

Silence again.

Her mom finally pulled the car to a stop in their driveway, shifting into park but not turning off the engine.

The dashboard lights painted their faces in soft amber tones.

"Come inside," she said gently.

Mariana didn't move.

"I will. In a second."

Her mom studied her for a long moment, then reached over and placed a hand on her daughter's knee. When she spoke again, her voice had lost its edge, revealing the worry underneath the anger.

"You're not a bad person, Mariana. And I know you didn't mean for any of this to happen. But being young doesn't protect you from consequences. Neither does being sorry." She squeezed Mariana's knee. "We survive by being careful, mi amor. By making good choices. By protecting each other."

Mariana nodded slowly. "I know."

"I trust you. Even now. But trust is something we carry — not something we drop and pick up like a bag."

Mariana's throat tightened. "He's a good guy, Mom. I need you to believe that."

Her mother hesitated, studying her daughter's face. "For you to care this much... maybe he is." She sighed. "Okay."

She opened her door, stepped out, and closed it softly behind her.

Mariana sat alone in the car, staring at the dark windshield, her reflection barely visible.

The house lights flickered on inside.

She didn't move.

She just whispered into the silence:

"Where are you, Richey?"

Morning After

Saturday morning arrived with harsh clarity, the kind that feels like punishment after a night that changed everything. Sunlight sliced through the blinds in Mariana's bedroom, cutting across her face. She hadn't closed them properly the night before. She hadn't done much of anything properly after coming home.

Her eyes felt swollen, gritty from crying and too little sleep. She blinked at the ceiling, the events of the previous night crashing back into her consciousness like waves against rocks. The party. Richey. Their conversation. The kiss. And then—chaos. Screaming. Him running. The car.

Where is he now?

She reached for her phone on the nightstand, checking for messages. Nothing from Daniel. Nothing from anyone who might know something. Just a string of texts from teammates about today's practice, oblivious to her world collapsing.

Her door creaked open. Vanessa peeked in, already dressed in jeans and a hoodie despite the early hour.

"Hey," Vanessa whispered, stepping inside and closing the door behind her. "You awake?"

Mariana sat up, pushing tangled hair from her face. "Yeah."

Vanessa sat on the edge of the bed, studying her sister's face. There was no teasing this morning, no sisterly jabs about being home early

129

from the party. Just concern.

"Mom's making breakfast," Vanessa said. "She told Dad you came home early because you weren't feeling well."

Mariana's eyes widened slightly. "She did?"

Vanessa nodded. "I think she's waiting to see what you want to say."

The weight of her mother's discretion hit Mariana with unexpected force. It wasn't forgiveness—not exactly. But it was space. Room to breathe, to figure out what came next.

"Thanks," Mariana said, voice barely audible.

"I heard you crying last night," Vanessa said, picking at a loose thread on the comforter. "What happened?"

Mariana pulled her knees to her chest, that hollow feeling returning to her stomach.

"Everything went wrong," she began, the words catching in her throat. "Jackie was drunk and started screaming about Richey being upstairs with me. But we were just talking, Vanessa. Nothing happened. He was... he was actually really nice."

She swallowed hard, remembering the way he'd spoken to her, how she'd felt seen for the first time in forever.

"And then he ran out because Jackie was yelling, and he took Daniel's car, and—" Her voice broke.

"And what?" Vanessa prompted gently.

"And I don't know where he is," Mariana finished, the tears threatening again. "He just drove off. He was upset. What if something happened to him?"

Vanessa reached over to squeeze her hand. "Have you tried calling Daniel?"

"Not yet. I don't even have his number. We're not really friends, we just—"

A soft knock at the door interrupted them. Their mother stood in the doorway, still in her robe, hair tied back in a loose bun. Her expression was carefully neutral, but the shadows under her eyes suggested she hadn't slept much either.

"Girls," she said softly. "Breakfast is ready."

She looked at Mariana, a silent question in her eyes. *Are you ready to talk about it?*

"I'll be down in a minute, Mom," Mariana said, trying to keep her voice steady.

Her mother nodded, lingering for a moment. "Take your time. Your father's reading the paper. It's just us this morning."

After she left, Mariana dragged herself out of bed. Every movement felt heavy, like she was swimming through something thicker than water.

"You can borrow my blue sweater," Vanessa offered, already moving toward her closet. "The soft one. It might make you feel better."

Mariana managed a weak smile. "Thanks."

Vanessa nodded slowly. 'So, this is definitely not how I expected your birthday weekend to go,' she said, attempting lightness.

'Though you have to admit, it's dramatic enough for your personality.'

Mariana smile was dim and burdened. She knew Vanessa just wanted to cheer her up. There was just too much swirling in her head.

Twenty minutes later, she sat at the kitchen table, picking at a plate of eggs and toast. Her father had already gone to his workshop in the garage, giving the women of the house their space—another small mercy she hadn't expected. The kitchen was quiet except for the gentle scrape of forks against plates and the hum of the refrigerator.

Her mother sat across from her, sipping coffee, eyes occasionally drifting to Mariana's face.

"I should have told you," Mariana finally said, breaking the silence. "About the party. That Jackie's parents weren't home."

Her mother set down her mug. "Yes. You should have."

The simple agreement, free of lectures, somehow hurt more.

"I'm sorry," Mariana whispered. "I just wanted..." She trailed off, unable to articulate exactly what she'd been chasing.

"To be like the other girls?" her mother suggested. "To have fun without worrying about consequences?"

Mariana looked up, surprised at the lack of judgment in her mother's tone.

"Maybe," she admitted. "But it wasn't just that. I felt like I was drowning, Mom. Every day it's school and swimming and being perfect and making you proud and never messing up. And for once, I just wanted to breathe."

Her mother's eyes softened. "Oh, *mija*."

"And now Richey is gone, and I don't know where he is, and it's my fault because I fell asleep and—"

"Stop," her mother said firmly. "Whatever happened at that party, you did not force this boy to take someone else's car and drive away. That was his choice."

"But Jackie was screaming at him because of me. She thought he..." Mariana couldn't finish the sentence.

Her mother's expression darkened slightly. "Thought he what?"

"She thought he did something to me. But he didn't, Mom. We were just talking, and I fell asleep because I was so tired from the meet. He even covered me with a blanket. He was being nice." Her voice cracked. "And now everyone's going to think he's something he's not."

Her mother reached across the table and took her hand. "Mariana, listen to me. I am disappointed that you lied to me. That trust between us—that's important. But I'm also worried about you right now, and that matters more."

Mariana blinked back tears. "I need to know if he's okay."

Her mother seemed to be weighing something, making a decision.

"This boy," she said carefully. "Richey. Who is he to you?"

Mariana hesitated. "I don't know yet. But... he could be important."

Her mother nodded slowly. "Do you have a way to contact him?"

"No. But his friend Daniel might know where he is."

Vanessa, who had been quietly listening, suddenly stood up. "I can help with that. I have Jonathan's number from chemistry lab, and he's on the football team with Richey. I can text him."

Mariana looked at her sister gratefully. "Would you?"

Vanessa was already pulling out her phone. "Already on it."

Their mother watched this exchange with a mixture of concern and resignation.

"Mariana," she said, "whatever happened, however this turns out—you understand there will still be consequences for lying to us, yes?"

Mariana nodded. "I know."

"But first, we make sure everyone is safe," her mother said, standing and clearing the plates. "That's what matters most right now."

Mariana felt a rush of gratitude. Her mother wasn't overlooking what she'd done, but she was prioritizing what mattered in this moment. It was a kind of grace she hadn't expected.

Vanessa's phone buzzed, and her eyes widened as she read the message.

"What?" Mariana asked, heart racing. "What is it?"

Vanessa looked up slowly, face pale. "Jonathan says Richey was in an accident last night. He's in the hospital."

The room seemed to tilt. The air vanished from Mariana's lungs.

"What kind of accident?" her mother asked sharply, stepping closer.

"Car crash," Vanessa read. "He ran a red light and hit a truck. They don't know if..." She stopped, glancing worriedly at Mariana.

"If what?" Mariana demanded, her voice barely recognizable.

Vanessa swallowed. "If he's going to be okay. He's in intensive care."

Mariana's chair scraped against the floor as she stood abruptly. Her legs felt like they might give way. The room spun. This couldn't be happening. Not because of one party. Not because of her.

"Which hospital?" her mother asked, already reaching for her keys on the counter.

"Memorial County," Vanessa read from her phone.

Mariana looked at her mother, a silent plea in her eyes.

Her mother nodded once. "Get your coat. Let's go."

Hospitality

The hospital smelled like industrial cleaner and stale coffee. The fluorescent lights made everyone look sickly, casting harsh shadows under tired eyes. Mariana stood in the lobby, her mother's hand firm on her shoulder, as they approached the information desk. The constant hum of medical equipment and hushed conversations created a background rhythm that seemed to match her anxious heartbeat. The polished floor squeaked under her shoes with each step, the sound unnaturally loud in her heightened state of awareness.

"We're here about Richard Vance," her mother said, her accent slightly more pronounced when she was anxious. "He was brought in last night. Car accident."

The receptionist typed something into her computer, then looked up with practiced sympathy.

"Are you family?"

"No," her mother replied. "We're... friends."

The woman's expression closed slightly. "I'm sorry, but only immediate family is allowed in intensive care. You're welcome to wait, but I can't give you any information on his condition."

Mariana felt her throat tighten. "Please, we just need to know if he's okay."

"I understand," the woman said, not unkindly. "But those are the rules. You can leave your name, and if the family wants to share information, we can pass it along."

Mariana began to protest, but her mother squeezed her shoulder.

"We understand," her mother said. "Is the family here? His father?"

"I believe his father arrived early this morning," the receptionist said, glancing at her screen. "But that's all I can tell you."

Her mother nodded and guided Mariana toward the waiting area. They sat in uncomfortable chairs beneath a muted television showing weekend cartoons. The contrast between the colorful animation and the weight of this place was jarring.

"Now what?" Mariana asked, her voice small.

"Now we wait," her mother said. "And we pray."

Mariana hadn't prayed properly in a long time. Not the way her grandmother had taught her, with rosary beads and whispered devotions. But sitting there, under the buzz of fluorescent lights, she found herself forming words in her mind—fragmented pleas to anyone who might be listening.

Please let him be okay. Please don't let this be my fault. Please give us another chance.

Her phone buzzed. A text from Daniel.

Daniel: I heard ur at hospital. I'm coming. Wait for me.

She showed the message to her mother, who nodded.

"Good," she said. "Maybe he can tell us more."

Twenty minutes crawled by. Mariana watched the elevator doors, waiting for Daniel to appear. Instead, when the doors slid open, a different figure emerged.

A man with rumpled clothes and dark circles under bloodshot eyes. His hair was a mess, his jaw covered in stubble. He looked like he'd aged a decade overnight. But there was no mistaking who he was.

Richey's father.

He walked toward the coffee machine, movements mechanical, not noticing them. Mariana stood before she could think about what she was doing.

"Mr. Vance?"

He turned, confusion momentarily crossing his haggard face. "Yes?"

She stepped forward, heart hammering. "I'm Mariana. I'm... I was with Richey last night. Before the accident."

His expression hardened slightly, eyes narrowing as he took her in. "You're from the party."

It wasn't a question. Mariana nodded, suddenly aware of how this must look to him—this strange girl appearing in the hospital, claiming some connection to his son.

"How is he?" she asked, the words barely audible.

James Vance stared at her for a long moment. She couldn't read his expression—anger, confusion, exhaustion all blended together.

"He's alive," he finally said. The words were flat, emotionless. "That's about all I can say right now."

Mariana's mother stepped up beside her, placing a protective hand on her back.

"Mr. Vance, I'm Gloria Garcia, Mariana's mother," she said. "We're very sorry about what happened. If there's anything we can do..."

James let out a short, humorless laugh. "Unless you can turn back time or fix a punctured lung, I don't think there's much anyone can do."

Mariana felt the room spin again. *Punctured lung.* The words echoed in her head, making the situation suddenly, horribly real.

"I should..." James gestured vaguely toward the elevator. "I should get back up there."

"Of course," Gloria said. "We understand. But perhaps Mariana could leave her number? In case..."

James looked at Mariana again, this time with something like recognition flickering in his tired eyes.

"You're the swimmer," he said suddenly.

Mariana blinked in surprise. "Yes."

"He mentioned you," James said. "Before. Said you were good."

The simple statement hit her like a physical blow. Richey had talked about her to his father. She mattered enough to mention.

James reached into his pocket and pulled out an old flip phone. "Put your number in. If there's any change, I'll... I'll let you know."

With trembling fingers, Mariana entered her contact information. When she handed the phone back, their eyes met briefly. There was no forgiveness there, no absolution. But there was acknowledgment. A tired nod that said her presence here meant something.

"Thank you," she whispered.

James nodded once more, then turned and walked back to the elevator, shoulders hunched as if carrying a weight too heavy to bear.

As the doors closed behind him, Mariana felt her legs give way. Her mother guided her back to the chairs, arm firmly around her waist.

"Punctured lung," Mariana repeated, the medical term sterile and terrifying.

"He's alive," her mother reminded her, echoing James' words but with gentle insistence. "That's what matters now."

The elevator doors opened again, and this time Daniel emerged, looking almost as haggard as James. When he saw Mariana, relief spread across his face.

"You're here," he said, crossing to them quickly. "Have you heard anything? Is he—"

"We just spoke to his father," Gloria said. "He's alive, but in serious condition."

"Daniel sank into the chair beside Mariana, running his hands through his hair. His usually easygoing expression was gone, replaced with a haunted look Mariana had never seen on him before.

'This is so messed up,' he muttered, voice cracking slightly.

"My car. My cousin. That party. Everything," Daniel said, running his hands through his hair. "Coach gave me permission to miss Friday's football conditioning because of the track meet earlier that day. That's why I had my car instead of riding with the other guys."

He stared at his hands, which were trembling. 'He's my best friend, you know? Since we were kids. I should have stopped him. I tried to run after the car, but—' he broke off, blinking rapidly to hold back tears. 'We've been through everything together. He can't just—'"

Mariana turned to him, desperate for answers. "What happened, Daniel? After he left?"

Daniel shook his head, eyes haunted. "He was driving too fast. Ran a red light. Didn't see the truck coming through the intersection."

He looked at her, and for the first time, she saw anger beneath his worry.

"Why did Jackie freak out like that? What the hell happened upstairs?"

"Nothing," Mariana insisted. "We were just talking. I fell asleep. He was about to leave when Jackie found him. She jumped to conclusions, started screaming—"

Daniel cursed under his breath. "She always does this. Makes everything about drama. And now look what happened."

"It's not just her fault," Mariana said quietly. "It's mine too. I should have said something. Stopped him."

"You were asleep," Daniel pointed out.

"And you were trying to stop him," she countered. "I wasn't even there."

Gloria interrupted gently. "This isn't the time to assign blame. What's done is done. Now we need to focus on supporting Richey's recovery."

Daniel looked at Mariana's mother with newfound respect. "Yes, ma'am."

They sat in silence for a moment, the weight of the situation settling around them like heavy fog.

"There's more," Daniel finally said, voice low. "The police were here earlier. There might be charges. DUI, reckless driving, even grand theft auto since he took my car without permission."

Mariana's heart sank further. "But you wouldn't press charges, would you?"

"Of course not," Daniel said quickly. "But the other stuff... that's out of my hands."

Gloria squeezed Mariana's shoulder. "One thing at a time, *mija*. First, he needs to heal."

Mariana nodded, unable to speak past the lump in her throat. She thought of Richey as she'd last seen him—gentle, vulnerable, his fingers laced with hers. Now he was upstairs, broken and unconscious, tubes and machines keeping him alive.

And somehow, impossibly, this was only the beginning of what they would have to face.

The morning light streamed through the hospital windows, marking the start of a Saturday that should have been about celebration and possibility. Instead, it was the first day of whatever came after disaster—the long, uncertain path that none of them had chosen but all of them would have to walk.

Mariana leaned against her mother's shoulder, closing her eyes.

Please let him wake up. Please let him be okay. Please give us a chance to make this right.

The prayers continued, silent but insistent, as the hospital buzzed with life around them—a stark reminder that for everyone else, this was just another ordinary day.

The Weight of Water

James Vance pressed his forehead against the cool glass of the hospital window, watching Houston sprawl beneath the harsh midday sun. From the tenth floor, the city seemed deceptively peaceful—glinting glass towers, endless ribbons of highway, the distant shimmer of Buffalo Bayou winding through concrete and steel. Traffic moved below like blood through veins, everyone rushing somewhere important, lives uninterrupted by tragedy.

He'd been standing there for almost twenty minutes, unable to look back at the bed where his son lay motionless, swallowed by machines and tubes. The steady beep of monitors had become a kind of torture— each tone a reminder that Richey's life hung by the most fragile thread.

When he'd returned to the ICU after meeting that girl—Mariana— and her mother, the doctor had been waiting with updates. None of them good.

"The pressure on his brain isn't decreasing as quickly as we'd hoped," Dr. Mehta had explained, her face carefully neutral. "We've induced a coma to give his brain time to heal and reduce swelling."

James had nodded mechanically, the words washing over him like waves too powerful to fight.

"The punctured lung is stable for now, but we're monitoring closely. Three broken ribs. Fractured collarbone. Internal bleeding that we've managed to control." She'd paused, allowing each injury to land like a blow. "He's young and strong, Mr. Vance. That's in his favor."

Young. Strong. The words echoed hollowly now as James finally turned from the window to face his son.

Richey looked impossibly small in the hospital bed. Tubes snaked from his mouth, his arms, disappearing beneath the thin blanket. His face was swollen, mottled with bruises, a line of neat stitches tracking across his forehead like a signature of violence. The rhythmic rise and fall of his chest wasn't his own breathing—it was a machine doing the work his body couldn't manage.

James sank into the chair beside the bed, his legs finally giving out after hours of pacing.

"Richey," he whispered, his voice like sandpaper. "I don't know if you can hear me."

The machines beeped in response. A nurse moved quietly at the doorway, checking something on a chart before slipping away. They had become ghosts to each other, these hospital staff, moving around him with practiced invisibility.

James reached out, hesitating before placing his rough hand over his son's bruised one. When was the last time he'd touched Richey with gentleness? Not a clap on the shoulder or a push toward the door, but this—simple human contact, skin to skin?

"I messed up," he said. The words stuck in his throat, tangled in years of pride and bitterness. "I messed up so bad, son."

His eyes burned. His chest felt tight, as if his own lungs were punctured, struggling for air.

"Your mom would..." He faltered, the mention of Eleanor still painful after all these years. Eleanor with her eyes like summer afternoons, her laugh that filled rooms. Eleanor who had finally had enough—of the drinking, the anger, the slow disintegration of the man she'd married. "Your mom would know what to say right now. She always did."

Outside, rain had begun to fall, streaking the window with diagonal lines. Houston weather, changeable as grief.

"I keep thinking about Bobby," James continued, his thumb tracing circles on the back of Richey's hand. "My brother. Your uncle. You don't remember him—you were too young. But he had this way of lighting up a room, making everyone feel like they mattered."

The memory surfaced with painful clarity—Bobby with his wide grin and easy charm, always the favorite, always the one who could talk his way out of trouble.

"When he died—" James's voice cracked. "When we lost him to that goddamn heroin, I promised myself I wouldn't end up like him. Wouldn't let chemicals take me out." A bitter laugh escaped him. "But here I am, killing myself just the same. Just slower. With whiskey instead of needles."

He squeezed Richey's hand, gently, mindful of the IV.

"And worse—I've been killing us. What we could have been. Father and son."

A sob broke loose then, raw and unexpected, tearing from somewhere deep inside him. James doubled over, still clutching Richey's hand, as years of suppressed emotion crashed through the walls he'd built.

"I'm sorry," he gasped between sobs. "God, I'm so sorry, Richey. For all of it. For not being there. For not seeing you. For making you feel like you had to run."

The monitors continued their steady rhythm, indifferent to his breakdown.

"Please," James whispered, looking up at his son's battered face. "Please don't go. Please stay and give me a chance to make it right. I'll do better. I swear on everything I have left, I'll do better."

He laid his head down on the edge of the bed, tears soaking into the thin hospital blanket. For how long he stayed there, he couldn't say. Time had become meaningless, measured only in beeps and breaths.

Eventually, a gentle hand on his shoulder roused him.

"Mr. Vance?" It was Nurse Calderon, the one who had called him in the middle of the night. Her eyes were kind, her voice low. "The doctor would like to speak with you again."

James straightened, wiping his face with his sleeve. "Is something wrong? Has something changed?"

"Dr. Mehta just wants to discuss the plan for the next 24 hours," she assured him. "And I think you could use a break. Have you eaten today?"

He shook his head, suddenly aware of the hollow ache in his stomach.

"There's a cafeteria on the second floor," she said. "We'll call you immediately if there's any change. But you need to take care of yourself too."

James nodded, standing stiffly. His body felt decades older than his forty-three years. He looked down at Richey once more, reached out to brush a strand of hair from his forehead.

"I'll be back soon," he promised. "I'm not going far."

James Vance emerged from the elevator. He looked taken back at seeing Daniel, exhausted. He faintly smiled and nodded in recognition.

"Mr. Vance," Daniel said, stepping forward. "How is he?"

"The same," James replied. "Doctors say the next twenty-four hours are critical."

Daniel hesitated, then asked, "Could I... would it be okay if I saw him? Just for a minute?"

James studied the boy's face, noting the genuine concern there. "Of course. Room 214. I have to head out for a bit but ill be right back, call me if anything happens."

Daniel nodded gratefully and headed for the elevator.

Inside Room 214, the steady beep of monitors greeted him. Daniel stopped in the doorway, momentarily paralyzed by the sight of Richey—tubes, wires, bandages, his usually expressive face now slack and unresponsive.

"Man..." he whispered, approaching the bed slowly. "What did you do, Rich?"

He pulled the visitor's chair closer, sitting awkwardly at first, then leaning forward with his elbows on his knees.

"So, this is messed up," he said quietly. "You in here like this. Me out there trying to explain to everyone what happened."

Daniel ran a hand through his hair, his typical easygoing manner replaced by genuine distress.

"Remember in seventh grade when I got that concussion at soccer practice? You visited every day for two weeks. Brought me homework—which I definitely didn't want—but also those terrible sci-fi movies we'd stay up watching."

He reached out timidly, then placed his hand on Richey's arm.

"You've been there for all the important stuff, you know? When my grandpa died. When I choked during track finals last year. You've always been the steady one." His voice cracked slightly. "I need you to be steady now, Rich. I need you to fight."

Daniel glanced toward the door, making sure he was alone, then continued more softly.

"You know what's funny? I always thought I was the outgoing one—parties, people, all that. But you're the brave one. Always have been. Standing up to Patrick in fourth grade. Taking on Chad in the locker room. You see something that needs doing, and you just... do it."

He swallowed hard, blinking rapidly.

"The team's asking about you. Coach is holding your spot. Everyone's pulling for you." He leaned closer. "And Mariana—she's been here since it happened. Hasn't left except when they made her. She really cares, man."

The monitors beeped steadily, the only response to Daniel's words.

"I should have stopped you," he whispered. "I ran after the car, but you were already gone. I should have grabbed the keys earlier or—" He broke off, shaking his head. "I'm sorry, Rich. This wasn't supposed to happen."

A nurse appeared in the doorway. "Just need to check his vitals," she said softly.

Daniel nodded and stood. "I'll be back, okay? Every day until you wake up. That's what best friends do."

He squeezed Richey's arm once more, then stepped back to let the nurse work.

"Stay strong, brother," he said at the door. "We've still got senior year to crush."

Clean House

The drive home felt like navigating a foreign country. James moved through Houston's Saturday afternoon traffic in a daze, the familiar landmarks of his daily commute transformed by grief into something strange and hostile.

He passed the exit for Memorial High School, where the marquee still announced next Saturdays game against Westfield. A game Richey could very well have started. The thought twisted in his gut like a knife.

The radio stayed off. He couldn't bear news or music or chattering DJs with their weekend enthusiasm. The silence in the cab of his truck was broken only by the rhythmic swish of windshield wipers battling the steady drizzle.

Houston unfurled around him—the sprawling city he'd called home his entire life. They'd lived in better neighborhoods once, before the divorce, before Eleanor took half of everything and his drinking ate through the rest. Now home was the tired little house in a forgotten corner of the city, where chain-link fences protected patches of yellowed grass, and front porches sagged with neglect.

The doctors had insisted he go home—shower, eat something substantial, collect some things for Richey. Maybe sleep, though he'd laughed at that suggestion. Sleep felt like a betrayal when Richey couldn't wake up.

As he turned onto his street, the house came into view like an accusation. Peeling paint. Gutters clogged with leaves. The crooked mailbox Richey had fixed three times, only to have James back into it again during one of his drunken returns from the bar.

He pulled into the driveway, killed the engine, and sat there, rain drumming on the roof. The house had never looked more like what it was—not a home, but a shelter for his slow surrender. A place where he'd nursed resentments instead of relationships, where he'd let his son grow up surrounded by the wreckage of his father's failures.

When he finally stepped inside, the smell hit him first—stale cigarettes, spilled beer, unwashed dishes. The television was still on, muted infomercials flickering in the dim light. Empty bottles cluttered the coffee table. An ashtray overflowed onto a water-ringed coaster.

James stood in the center of the living room, seeing it all through new eyes—through Richey's eyes. The boy had grown up in this. This chaos, this neglect, this monument to giving up.

"Jesus Christ," he whispered, the sound absorbed by the silence of the house.

He moved to the kitchen, flipped on the light. More bottles lined the counter. The refrigerator hummed, nearly empty save for condiments and a six-pack. The sink held days of unwashed dishes, a film of grease congealing on the surface of stagnant water.

His gaze landed on the cabinet above the refrigerator—his private stash. Three bottles of whiskey, the good stuff, reserved for what he called "real bad days." As if any day in recent memory had been good.

Something snapped inside him.

He yanked open the cabinet, grabbed the first bottle—Jack Daniel's, half-empty. The cap came off with practiced ease. Without hesitation, he tilted it over the sink, watching amber liquid swirl down the drain. The sharp scent of alcohol rose up, familiar and sickening.

Another bottle followed. Then the third.

He moved methodically through the house then, hunting down every hidden source of poison. The vodka behind the bathroom towels. The emergency flask in his nightstand. The beers in the garage refrigerator. All of it, down the drain, the bottles stacked beside the sink like trophies of war.

When he was finished, he stood breathing hard, staring at the empty containers. How many paychecks had he poured away? How many conversations with his son had he missed, too numb to engage? How many mornings had Richey woken to find his father passed out, unreachable?

"Eleanor," he whispered, his ex-wife's name a prayer and a lament. "Bobby. I'm so damn sorry."

Eleanor Cassidy Vance had been everything bright in his life—a kindergarten teacher with endless patience, a woman who saw potential in everyone, even a rough-edged machinist with trust issues and a chip on his shoulder. She'd tried so hard, for so long, to help him face Bobby's death, to process the grief that had calcified into rage. But in the end, she'd had to save herself. Had to save Richey from growing up watching his father disappear one bottle at a time.

And Bobby—his wild, brilliant younger brother—dead at twenty-four from an overdose in some filthy apartment while James was working a double shift. The guilt had eaten him alive. The what-ifs. The could-have-beens.

Now Richey lay in a hospital bed, another chance James might lose because he hadn't been the father his son deserved.

Not this time.

James moved with sudden purpose, grabbing garbage bags from under the sink. He filled them rapidly—empty bottles, cigarette packs, the overflowing ashtray, takeout containers crusted with forgotten meals. He tied off one bag, started another, working with the desperate energy of a man trying to outrun his own shadow.

He stripped the couch of cushions, finding coins, remote controls, more cigarette butts. He pulled the curtains open for the first time in months, letting gray daylight flood the room. Dust motes swirled in the sudden brightness, disturbed after years of settlement.

In the kitchen, he tackled the sink, scrubbing dishes until his hands were raw. The counter emerged from beneath its layer of grime. The stovetop revealed itself, one wiped section at a time.

He worked without stopping, without thinking, moving from room to room like a man possessed. The bathroom. The hallway. His bedroom, with its rumpled sheets and clothes strewn across the floor. The corner where he'd tossed his steel-toed work boots and the lunch cooler he carried to the machine shop every morning.

Finally, he reached Richey's room.

He paused at the threshold, hand on the doorknob. When was the last time he'd entered this space? When was the last time he'd respected it as his son's sanctuary?

The door swung open on quiet hinges. Unlike the rest of the house, Richey's room was neat—almost painfully so. Bed made with military precision. Books stacked on the desk, organized by subject. A small collection of football trophies arranged by size on a shelf Richey had built himself.

James stepped inside, feeling like a trespasser. This ordered space was a rebellion against the chaos just outside the door. A statement: *I am not you. I will not become you.*

He moved to the window, pulled open the blinds. Richey's view was of the neighbor's fence, a sliver of sky between rooftops. Not much of a vista, but it was something other than darkness.

On the desk sat a framed photograph—the only personal touch in the spartan room. James picked it up, his chest tightening. Eleanor holding a seven-year-old Richey on her lap, both of them laughing at something out of frame. It had been taken during one of her weekend visits, after the divorce but before she moved east with her new husband.

"I let him think you abandoned him," James whispered to Eleanor's smiling image. "Let him believe you didn't care, when it was me who pushed you away. Me who made it impossible."

He set the photo down carefully, noticing for the first time a slip of paper tucked into the edge of the frame. He hesitated, then gently pulled it free.

It was an old-style paper fortune from a Chinese restaurant, the kind they'd gotten on family nights out when things were better. The faded print read: *Your path may be difficult, but will lead to immense joy.*

James sank onto the edge of Richey's bed, the fortune trembling between his fingers.

His son had kept this. All these years. A small token of hope in a house where hope had been the first casualty.

"I'm going to fix this," James said aloud, folding the fortune and putting it back exactly where Richey had kept it. "Whatever it takes."

He stood, surveying the room once more, then returned to his cleaning mission with renewed focus. The house would be different when Richey came home. James would be different. It was the only gift he could offer now—the father his son deserved, the man Eleanor had once believed he could be.

Hours later, exhausted and aching, James Vance stood in his transformed living room. The old couch had been scrubbed as clean as possible. Windows gleamed. Floors emerged from beneath layers of neglect. The air smelled of lemon cleaner instead of stale smoke.

It wasn't enough. Not even close. But it was a beginning.

He showered, the hot water sluicing away sweat and grime, and dressed in the cleanest clothes he could find—jeans without stains, a button-down shirt Eleanor had bought him years ago, still hanging in the back of his closet. He packed a small bag for Richey—a toothbrush, the soft T-shirt he slept in, a dog-eared paperback from his nightstand.

Before leaving, James paused in the kitchen, looking at the row of empty bottles he'd lined up like fallen soldiers. A reminder of what he was fighting.

He picked up his phone and, with trembling fingers, searched for something he'd deleted years ago. The contact was still there in his backup list: *AA - Mike P.*

Mike had been after him for years to get help, had kept reaching out long after James stopped returning calls. Had never given up, even when James had given up on himself.

James hit the call button before he could change his mind.

It rang three times before a gruff voice answered.

"Mike Patterson."

"Mike," James said, his voice catching. "It's James. James Vance."

A pause. "Well, I'll be damned. James Vance. Been a while, buddy."

"Yeah." James swallowed hard. "Listen, I—I need help, Mike. My son is in the hospital. Car accident. And I—I can't do this anymore. The drinking. I can't."

Another pause, longer this time. "I'm real sorry about your boy, James. Really am. But I'm proud of you for making this call. That takes guts."

James closed his eyes, fighting back tears. "I don't have any guts, Mike. I'm just terrified. Of losing him. Of what I've already lost."

"Fear's not a bad place to start," Mike said gently. "As long as you start. There's a meeting tonight at St. Mark's. Seven o'clock. I'll save you a seat."

"I can't tonight," James said. "I need to be at the hospital. But tomorrow. I'll be there tomorrow."

"Tomorrow works. I'll be there." Mike's voice softened. "One day at a time, James. That's all any of us can do."

"One day at a time," James repeated, the words strange on his tongue.

After hanging up, he gathered Richey's bag and his car keys. The rain had stopped, leaving Houston glossy and subdued in the late afternoon light. The subtropical humidity hung heavy, but for once, James didn't mind. It felt like being enveloped, held together by something larger than himself.

He locked the door behind him—a house transformed, if only superficially. The real work, the hardest work, was just beginning. But for the first time in years, James Vance stepped into the world without the weight of surrender pressing him down.

In his pocket, his fingers brushed against Richey's fortune. *Your path may be difficult, but will lead to immense joy.*

He could only hope those words might still come true for his son. And maybe, if he fought hard enough, for himself as well.

Collision Course

The hospital cafeteria had cleared out after the dinner rush, leaving behind the smell of industrial cleaning products barely masking microwaved food. Mariana sat at a corner table, picking at a styrofoam cup of vanilla pudding she'd bought just to have something to do with her hands. Her mother sat beside her, sipping tea that had long gone cold. They'd been at the hospital for hours, waiting for news, for permission, for something that felt like progress.

Daniel paced near the vending machines, phone pressed to his ear, his voice a tense murmur. He'd been making calls all afternoon—to his parents, to his older brothers, to Coach Kenneck. The same information, delivered over and over: Richey was critical but stable. The car was totaled. Yes, the police were involved.

The double doors swung open, and Mariana looked up, hoping for another update from Nurse Calderon. Instead, two uniformed police officers walked in, scanning the nearly empty cafeteria. One was tall and lean with close-cropped salt-and-pepper hair; the other shorter, stockier, with a thick mustache and tired eyes.

"That's him," the taller officer said, nodding toward Daniel. "The vehicle owner."

Daniel looked up, color draining from his face. He quickly ended his call.

"Officers," he said, straightening. "I was just about to come find you."

The stockier officer—his nameplate read RAMIREZ—gestured to a nearby table. "Mind if we sit down? We have some questions to get through."

Daniel glanced at Mariana, a silent plea in his eyes. She stood immediately, her mother following suit.

"This is Mariana Garcia," Daniel said, gesturing to her as the officers approached. "She was at the party last night. And her mother, Mrs. Garcia."

Officer Ramirez nodded politely. "Ma'am. I'm Officer Ramirez, this is Officer Thornton. We're handling the accident investigation."

"Is Richey in trouble?" Mariana asked, unable to stop herself.

The officers exchanged a look.

"That's what we're trying to determine," Officer Thornton said diplomatically. "We'd like to get statements from everyone who was present before the accident."

They all moved to a larger table. Mariana's stomach twisted as she sat down, feeling suddenly like she was about to be interrogated. Her mother placed a steady hand on her arm.

"We understand this is a difficult time," Officer Ramirez began, pulling out a small notebook. "But we need to establish a timeline. Daniel, you've already given us the basics, but we'd like to hear from Ms. Garcia as well."

Mariana swallowed hard. "What do you need to know?"

"Start with yesterday evening," Officer Thornton said. "When did you arrive at the party?"

"Around seven," Mariana said. "After my swim meet. Jackie—it was her house—picked me up from school."

"And the party was unsupervised? No parents present?"

Mariana glanced at her mother, then nodded. "Jackie's parents were supposed to be there, but their flight got delayed."

"There was alcohol being served?"

"Some," she admitted. "Jackie's cousin brought it. I only had one cup."

Daniel shifted uncomfortably.

"And what time did Richard Vance arrive?" Officer Ramirez asked.

"I don't know exactly. Maybe eight-thirty? Nine?"

"Was he drinking?"

Mariana tried to remember. "I think he had something in his hand when he came in, but I didn't see him drink much."

"And what led to him leaving in such a hurry?" Officer Thornton leaned forward.

Mariana hesitated, shame coloring her cheeks. "We were upstairs talking. Just talking. I fell asleep—I was exhausted from my meet. When I woke up, everything was chaotic. Jackie had... misunderstood the situation."

"Misunderstood how?" Ramirez pressed.

"She thought—" Mariana's voice caught. "She thought something inappropriate had happened while I was asleep. But nothing did. Richey was just there. He was being nice."

"She started yelling at him," Daniel interjected. "Accusing him. Everyone heard. He panicked and ran out."

"And drove away in your car," Officer Thornton noted.

"Yeah," Daniel said, running a hand through his hair. "We drove together to the party. My brother dropped us at Daniel's house, and we took my car from there. I let Richey hold onto the keys since his jacket had actual pockets." He looked down. "I never thought he'd just take off in it."

"Blood tests from the hospital show his blood alcohol at 0.04," Officer Ramirez said. "Below the legal limit for an adult, but he's sixteen. Any amount is a violation of zero-tolerance laws."

Gloria spoke up for the first time. "He's a child who made a terrible mistake," she said firmly. "He's already paying a devastating price."

The cafeteria doors swung open again. This time, three young men entered—all with Daniel's same features but older, more serious. The tallest one spotted them and made a beeline for their table.

"Daniel," he called out. "What the hell is going on?"

Officer Thornton stood. "And you are?"

"Marcus Patterson. Daniel's oldest brother. "Our parents are in Austin on business. I'm handling this until they get back."

Marcus looked to be in his mid-twenties, dressed in slacks and a rumpled dress shirt, as if he'd come straight from work at the law firm where he was a paralegal. A real expression of concern and irritation. Unlike Andrew, who had followed the academic path, or their parents, who ran the family restaurant, Marcus had chosen a more corporate direction.

"Your brother's car was involved in a serious accident," Officer Thornton explained.

"I know that," Marcus snapped. "What I don't know is why my sixteen-year-old brother was at an unsupervised party with alcohol, or why his car is now wrecked on Morrison Avenue."

"It was T-boned at an intersection," Daniel corrected him. "Truck hit the passenger side when Richey ran a red light."

Marcus ran his hand through his hair. "Whatever. The point is, the car is totaled."

Officer Ramirez stepped in. "Sir, we're in the middle of taking statements. If you'd like to join us, you're welcome to, but—"

The doors opened yet again, this time with more force. James Vance strode in, freshly showered but still haggard, his eyes immediately locking on the cluster of police and teenagers.

"What's happening here?" he demanded, approaching the table. "I go home for two hours, and you're interrogating kids while my son is upstairs fighting for his life?"

Officer Thornton turned to face him. "Mr. Vance. We're just gathering information about the circumstances leading to the accident."

James's jaw tightened. "Have you been to see him? Have you seen what he looks like right now? He's sixteen years old, for God's sake."

"We understand this is difficult—" Officer Ramirez began.

"No, you don't," James cut him off. "You have no idea. Go ahead and ticket him. Charge him. Whatever you need to do. But can it wait until he's at least conscious?"

An uncomfortable silence fell over the group. Mariana studied James's face, noticing the redness around his eyes, the new clarity in them. He looked different from the broken man she'd met earlier—still devastated, but with something like purpose in his stance.

Marcus stepped forward, extending a hand. "Mr. Vance? I'm Marcus Patterson, Daniel's brother. I want you to know we're not pressing charges for the car. That's the least of our concerns right now."

James looked at the offered hand for a moment before taking it. "Thank you," he said gruffly. "But there's still property damage. The truck. The streetlight."

"The truck driver isn't pressing charges either," Officer Thornton informed them. "He's concerned about the boy. Said accidents happen, especially to young drivers."

"What about his insurance?" James asked, running a hand through his damp hair. "I'll cover whatever his deductible is. I'll figure something out."

He glanced down at his calloused hands, a machinist's hands, wondering how many extra shifts he could pick up at the plant to cover the mounting medical bills.

"Dad's already handling the insurance angle," Marcus Patterson added. "The car was under his policy."

Mariana caught the brief flash of relief on James's face. One less impossible burden.

Officer Ramirez cleared his throat. "Mr. Vance, we still need to complete our investigation. There are potential charges—DUI under zero tolerance laws, reckless driving, running a red light. But the DA will take the circumstances into account, especially given Richard's current condition."

"His name is Richey," James corrected quietly. "Nobody calls him Richard except teachers."

The small detail seemed to soften something in the room, a reminder that they were discussing a real person, not just a case number.

The cafeteria doors opened once more. Jackie entered, followed by a man and woman who could only be her parents—both dressed in business casual, expressions tight with concern. Jackie spotted Mariana immediately, her step faltering.

"Oh no," Daniel muttered.

Jackie approached cautiously, her parents trailing behind her. She looked nothing like the party girl from last night—her face scrubbed clean of makeup, hair pulled back, eyes red-rimmed.

"Mariana," she said hesitantly. "I came as soon as I heard how bad it was."

Mariana felt a surge of emotions—anger, hurt, confusion. "How could you not know how bad it was? He took off because of what you said."

Jackie flinched. "I was drunk. I just saw you passed out and him leaving the room, and I freaked out. I didn't think—"

"That's right," Mariana snapped, rising from her chair. "You didn't think. You just started screaming accusations in front of everyone."

"Who's this?" James asked, looking between the girls.

"Jackie Miller," Daniel supplied. "It was her party. She's the one who... misunderstood the situation."

Understanding dawned on James's face, followed by a flash of anger. Before he could speak, Jackie's father stepped forward.

"I'm Robert Miller," he said, directing his words to the officers. "This was at our home? While we were out of town?"

Officer Thornton nodded. "It appears so, sir."

Robert turned to his daughter. "Jackie, you told us it was just a few girls for a sleepover. You specifically said your mother and I would be home before any visitors arrived."

Jackie looked at the floor. "I know. I'm sorry."

Her mother placed a hand on her shoulder. "We'll discuss this at home," she said tightly. Then, to the room at large: "We're here because our daughter has something to say."

Jackie took a shaky breath. "I need to tell the police what really happened," she said. "It wasn't Richey's fault. I accused him of... taking advantage of Mariana while she was asleep. But that's not what happened. I jumped to conclusions and started yelling, and everyone was watching, and he ran out."

Officer Ramirez made notes. "So in your view, his flight from the scene was prompted by false accusations?"

"Yes," Jackie said miserably. "He looked terrified. Like he was being hunted."

James made a small, pained sound.

Mariana felt tears springing to her eyes. She remembered Richey's face in those final moments at the party—the panic, the hurt. The sense that no one would believe him. She couldn't stop imagining what must have been going through his mind as he drove, too fast and too reckless, through rain-slicked streets.

"Will this help?" Gloria asked the officers. "Knowing that he wasn't just being irresponsible, but was reacting to a traumatic situation?"

Officer Thornton sighed. "It provides context. The DA will take it into consideration. But the fact remains that he made the choice to drive after consuming alcohol, and he ran a red light."

"He's already got a punctured lung and brain swelling," James said, his voice strained. "Isn't that punishment enough?"

"The law doesn't work that way, Mr. Vance," Officer Ramirez said gently. "But we're not heartless. No one wants to see the boy suffer more than he already is."

The tension in the room was thick enough to touch. Mariana watched as James struggled visibly with his emotions—anger, fear, and something else she couldn't quite name.

"Can I ask something?" Daniel ventured. "If no one is pressing charges for the car or the truck damage, and everyone agrees this was... complicated... what exactly are you investigating for?"

The officers exchanged glances.

"Standard procedure in any accident with serious injuries," Officer Thornton said. "And the state can still pursue DUI charges regardless of whether individuals press charges."

"But you'll include everything in your report?" Gloria pressed. "About the circumstances? The misunderstanding?"

"We'll be thorough," Officer Ramirez assured her.

Jackie stepped closer to Mariana. "I'm so sorry," she whispered. "I never meant for any of this to happen."

Mariana couldn't bring herself to respond. Part of her wanted to scream at Jackie, to blame her for everything. Another part knew this chain of events couldn't be laid at any one person's feet.

"I should get back upstairs," James said, checking his watch. "Visitation hours end soon."

Officer Thornton nodded. "We'll need to speak with you again, Mr. Vance. And with Richey, when he's able."

"If he's able," James corrected, the fear naked in his voice.

"When," Mariana insisted, meeting James's eyes. "When he's able."

Something passed between them then—a fragile thread of hope, of mutual understanding. James nodded slightly, gratitude flickering across his exhausted face.

"We'll also need formal statements from both of you," Officer Ramirez said, gesturing to Mariana and Daniel. "And from you, Miss Miller."

Jackie nodded miserably. "Whatever you need."

As the group began to disperse, tensions still simmering beneath strained politeness, James paused beside Mariana.

"He talks about you," he said quietly. "More than just mentioning you're good at swimming. He notices things. Said you always have color-coded notes in class. Said you bite your lip when you're thinking hard about something."

Mariana's heart clenched. "I didn't know."

"Neither did I, until recently," James admitted. "I haven't been much for listening." He hesitated. "Do you want to see him? Before visiting hours end?"

Mariana glanced at her mother, who nodded encouragement.

"Yes," she said. "Please."

As they headed for the elevator, Marcus Patterson approached, holding out a business card.

"Mr. Vance," he said. "My father's insurance will cover the car, but there may be other expenses. Medical bills, legal fees." He gestured to the card. "I'm a paralegal at Brenner and Associates. We have people who handle cases like this. Pro bono sometimes, for the right situation."

James stared at the card. "I can't afford—"

"Just take it," Marcus said firmly. "Call if you need help navigating the system. No obligation."

James hesitated, then accepted the card, tucking it into his pocket. "Thank you."

In the elevator, Mariana stood beside James, their reflections ghostly in the brushed metal doors. So much had happened in less than twenty-four hours. Lives had been altered, trajectories changed. And at the center of it all was Richey, lying silent and still in his hospital bed.

"I keep thinking," James said suddenly, his voice low enough that only Mariana could hear, "about what must have been going through his head. To make him drive like that."

Mariana stared at their distorted reflections. "He was scared," she said softly. "Not of the police or getting in trouble. He was scared of being seen as someone he's not."

James nodded slowly. "He gets that from his mother. She couldn't stand being misunderstood either."

The elevator dinged, doors sliding open to reveal the ICU floor. As they stepped out, Mariana felt the weight of where they were heading—toward a room where machines breathed for Richey, where his future hung in a precarious balance.

"I don't know if this helps," she said, stopping James with a gentle touch on his arm, "but what I saw last night, before everything went wrong, was someone kind. Someone careful with his words. Someone who listened like what I had to say actually mattered."

James's eyes glistened. "That sounds like the son I haven't let myself see in a long time."

They continued down the hall in silence, toward Room 214, where the steady rhythm of machines marked each second that Richey remained in his forced sleep. Behind them, the elevator closed on the chaos they'd temporarily escaped—the questions, the accusations, the legal implications still to be faced.

But for now, for these last few minutes of visiting hours, there was only this: two people who cared about Richey, watching over him, each holding their own version of hope that when he finally opened his eyes, there would be a chance to make things right.

Silent Heartbeats

The ICU corridor stretched before them like a tunnel of muted light and hushed voices. Mariana followed James, her footsteps careful and measured, as if making too much noise might somehow disturb the fragile balance of healing taking place behind closed doors. The rhythmic beeping of monitors and the soft hiss of ventilators created a strange symphony—the sound of lives suspended between crisis and recovery.

Room 214 was at the end of the hall. James paused outside, his hand resting on the door handle. For a moment, he seemed unable to move forward.

"It's not easy," he said quietly. "Seeing him like this."

Mariana nodded, her throat tight. "I understand."

"No, you don't," he replied, not unkindly. "Not yet. But... thank you for coming anyway."

He pushed the door open, and the steady beep-beep-beep of Richey's heart monitor greeted them. The room was dimly lit, a single overhead light casting shadows across medical equipment and the still form on the bed. The air smelled of antiseptic and something else—something clinical and yet intimate, like the scent of someone's life force being carefully maintained by machines. The steady beep-beep-beep of Richey's heart monitor created a metronomic backdrop to their conversation, occasionally joined by the soft whoosh of the ventilator pushing air into his lungs. The room was too cold, as if designed to preserve rather than comfort, and Mariana fought the urge to rub her arms against the chill. A thin beam of afternoon light cut through the partially closed blinds, highlighting particles of dust floating in the still air.

Mariana stopped just inside the doorway, unprepared for what she saw.

Richey lay motionless beneath a thin blanket, his body seeming smaller somehow than she remembered from just yesterday. A breathing tube protruded from his mouth, secured with tape. His face was swollen and bruised, one eye blackened, the line of stitches across his forehead stark against his pale skin. His right arm was immobilized in a cast, and various tubes and wires connected him to machines that blinked and hummed with mechanical vigilance.

This wasn't the boy who had listened to her stories in Jackie's guest room, whose fingers had intertwined with hers, whose shy smile had made her feel seen. This was a broken vessel, its inhabitant somewhere far away.

James moved to the bedside with practiced caution, adjusting the blanket slightly, brushing a strand of hair from Richey's forehead with surprising gentleness.

"The nurse said talking to him might help," he said. "Even if he can't respond. They think he might be able to hear us."

Mariana stepped closer, her eyes never leaving Richey's face. "What do you say to him?"

James sat in the chair beside the bed. "Everything I should have said before. How proud I am. How sorry I am." He shrugged helplessly. "Sometimes I just talk about normal things. The weather. What's happening in the world. As if..."

"As if nothing's changed," Mariana finished.

"Yeah."

She stood on the opposite side of the bed, hesitant to touch Richey but desperate to establish some connection. Finally, she reached out and gently placed her hand next to his on the blanket, not quite touching but close enough to feel the warmth radiating from his skin.

"Hi, Richey," she said softly. "It's Mariana."

James watched her, his expression a mixture of gratitude and grief.

"I don't know if you can hear me," she continued, her voice gaining a little strength. "But I wanted you to know that I'm here. And I'm sorry about what happened at the party. Jackie told the police the truth—that nothing happened. That you didn't do anything wrong."

The machines continued their steady rhythm, indifferent to her words.

"Your dad's been here the whole time," she added, glancing at James. "And Daniel's been waiting downstairs. Even Coach Kenneck called to check on you."

James cleared his throat. "The team sent a card," he said, gesturing to a folded piece of paper on the windowsill. "Chad brought it by earlier. Said they all signed it."

Mariana smiled faintly. "See? Everyone's pulling for you."

A comfortable silence fell between them, broken only by the mechanical chorus of the room. James looked exhausted, the lines in his face deeper under the harsh hospital lighting. But there was something different in his eyes from when she'd first met him that morning—a clarity, a presence that hadn't been there before.

"How long will he..." Mariana hesitated, unsure how to phrase the question.

"Stay in the coma?" James finished. "They don't know. The doctor said they'll try to reduce the sedation gradually over the next couple of days if the swelling in his brain continues to decrease."

"But he'll wake up," Mariana said. It wasn't quite a question, but it wasn't quite a statement either.

James looked at his son. "That's the hope. But they're... cautious about making promises."

Before Mariana could respond, the door opened. A woman in a white coat entered, a tablet in hand. She was in her fifties, with silver-streaked black hair pulled back in a neat bun and intelligent eyes behind rimless glasses.

"Mr. Vance," she said, nodding to James. "I'm Dr. Mehta. We met earlier."

"How is he?" James asked immediately, rising from his chair.

Dr. Mehta moved to check the monitors, her movements efficient but gentle. "His vitals are stable. The intracranial pressure has decreased slightly, which is what we want to see." She glanced at Mariana. "And you are?"

"Mariana Garcia," she said. "I'm... a friend."

Dr. Mehta nodded, making a note on her tablet. "I'm glad Richey has support. That matters in recovery." She turned back to James. "We've scheduled another scan for tomorrow morning to check the swelling. If it continues to improve, we can discuss reducing sedation."

"And if it doesn't?" James asked, his voice tight.

The doctor's expression remained professional but compassionate. "Then we maintain the current course until we see improvement. Richey is young and was in excellent physical condition before the accident. That's significantly in his favor."

James nodded, absorbing this. "The punctured lung?"

"Holding steady. The chest tube is functioning well." Dr. Mehta made another notation. "I've scheduled the orthopedic team to check his collarbone and wrist tomorrow as well."

"Thank you," James said. "For everything you're doing."

Dr. Mehta's professional demeanor softened slightly. "That's our job, Mr. Vance." She paused. "I understand the police were here earlier. If you need help navigating that aspect, the hospital has social workers who can assist."

"I'll keep that in mind."

After a few more checks of Richey's vitals, Dr. Mehta turned to leave. "Visiting hours officially end in fifteen minutes, but the night nurse might allow you a little longer. Just keep it quiet."

As the door closed behind her, James sank back into his chair, visibly drained.

"He's going to need surgery," he said, rubbing his face. "On his collarbone. Maybe the wrist too. And there's physical therapy after. Months of it." He looked up, his eyes suddenly lost. "I don't even know if our insurance covers all that. The paperwork's somewhere at home, but I haven't—"

His voice broke. He turned away, shoulders hunched, fighting for control.

Mariana stood frozen, uncertain what to do. This man was a stranger to her—Richey's father, yes, but someone she'd met only hours ago. Yet in this sterile room, with Richey lying between them, they were connected by something deeper than familiarity.

"Mr. Vance," she said softly. "James."

He didn't respond, his breathing ragged as he battled emotions too powerful to contain.

Mariana moved around the bed and, without overthinking, placed a gentle hand on his shoulder. "He's strong," she said. "You saw what Dr. Mehta said. His body knows how to fight."

James's shoulders shook. "What if it's not enough?" he whispered. "What if I've already failed him too many times, and this is—" He couldn't finish the thought.

"This isn't punishment," Mariana said firmly. "It's not karma or fate or whatever. It's an accident. A terrible accident that happened because of a whole chain of events that no one person caused."

James looked up at her, his eyes red-rimmed. "You sound like your mother."

"I'll take that as a compliment."

A small smile flickered across his face, then disappeared. "I keep thinking about all the time I wasted," he said. "All the mornings I was too hungover to drive him to practice. All the nights I fell asleep in front of the TV instead of asking about his day. All the games I missed because I couldn't pull myself together." His voice hardened with self-loathing. "What kind of father does that?"

"A human one," Mariana said simply. "One who's still here. Still trying."

James looked at Richey, tears falling freely now. "I poured it all out," he said. "Every bottle in the house. Down the drain. I cleaned everything. Opened the windows. Made the place look like... like a home instead of a prison." He wiped roughly at his face. "For when he comes back."

"That's good," Mariana said, feeling the weight of his confession. "That's really good."

"But what if he doesn't come back?" James's voice was barely audible. "What if I did all that, and he never—"

"Stop," Mariana interrupted, surprising herself with her firmness. "He will come back. Maybe not tomorrow or next week, but he will. And when he does, he's going to need you—the real you. Not perfect, maybe, but present. Trying."

James looked at her for a long moment, as if seeing something beyond her sixteen years. "You hardly know me," he said finally. "Why do you believe I can change?"

Mariana glanced at Richey. "Because he sees something in you worth loving. Even after everything. That tells me there's something there."

A soft knock at the door interrupted them. A nurse peeked in. "I'm sorry, but visiting hours are ending," she said apologetically.

James nodded, standing and wiping his face. "We're coming."

Mariana moved back to Richey's side. Without hesitation this time, she took his hand gently in hers, careful of the IV.

"I'll be back tomorrow," she promised quietly. "Rest and get stronger, okay? There's... there's so much more I want to talk about with you."

James stood on the other side of the bed, resting his hand on Richey's shoulder. For a moment, they formed a circle—father, son, and the girl who had somehow become a bridge between them.

"See you in the morning, son," James said. "I'm not going far."

They left the room together, the door closing behind them with a soft click. The corridor seemed even quieter now, the hospital settling into its nighttime rhythm. They walked in silence toward the elevator, both lost in their own thoughts.

As they prepared to leave, a nurse approached with a clipboard. 'Mr. Vance? We need to update the visitor permissions for ICU access.'

James looked confused. 'What do you mean?'

'Hospital policy normally restricts ICU visitors to immediate family,' she explained, 'but we do make exceptions when authorized by the patient's guardian.' She gestured to Mariana and Gloria. 'If you'd like to add specific visitors to the approved list, you can do that now.'

James didn't hesitate. 'Yes. The Garcia family. And Daniel Patterson.' He glanced at Mariana. 'Richey would want them here.'

The nurse nodded, making notes on her form. 'I'll update this in our system. They'll still need to follow visiting hour restrictions, but they won't be turned away at the desk.'"

When the doors opened, Mariana was surprised to see her mother still waiting in the lobby, reading a magazine that had probably been there since last Christmas. Gloria looked up, relief crossing her face when she saw them.

"I was beginning to worry," she said, standing and gathering her purse. "How is he?"

James answered before Mariana could. "The same. But the doctor says there's some improvement in the brain swelling."

Gloria nodded, studying James's face with the careful assessment of a mother who had seen many tears, both hidden and revealed. "That's something to hold onto, then," she said gently.

"Yes," James agreed. "It is."

Mariana watched this exchange with a strange sense of worlds colliding. Her mother—who had always been so careful about the company her daughters kept, so vigilant against bad influences—was speaking to James Vance with genuine compassion.

"We should get home," Gloria said to Mariana. "Your father will be wondering where we are, and Vanessa has been texting."

"Can we come back tomorrow?" Mariana asked, trying to keep the plea from her voice.

Gloria and James exchanged glances.

"If Mr. Vance doesn't mind," Gloria said carefully.

"Please," James said. "Come whenever you can. I think... I think it helps him, hearing different voices."

Gloria nodded. "Then we'll be back in the afternoon, after church."

As they prepared to leave, Mariana turned to James one last time. "You'll call if anything changes? Even during the night?"

"I will," he promised. "I have your number."

She hesitated, then impulsively reached out and squeezed his arm. "Try to get some sleep. Even just a little. He needs you strong."

James looked startled by the gesture, but a hint of warmth touched his exhausted eyes. "I'll try."

Gloria watched this interaction with an expression Mariana couldn't quite read—not disapproval, exactly, but careful assessment. As they walked toward the hospital exit, Mariana felt her mother's arm slip around her shoulders.

"That was kind," Gloria said softly. "What you did for him."

Mariana looked up, surprised. "For Richey?"

"For his father," Gloria clarified. "That man is carrying a mountain of guilt and fear. You gave him something to hold onto."

Mariana hadn't thought of it that way. "I just said what felt true."

Gloria smiled sadly. "Sometimes that's the kindest thing we can do."

They pushed through the revolving door into the cool night air, the parking lot a constellation of yellow lights and gleaming car hoods. The world outside seemed strangely normal, indifferent to the battles being fought in rooms like 214.

"Do you think he'll be okay?" Mariana asked, the question she'd been holding inside finally escaping. "Really okay?"

Gloria pulled her daughter closer as they walked to the car. "I don't know, *mija*. But I know that love has a power all its own. Sometimes it's the only medicine that matters."

As they drove away from the hospital, Mariana looked back at the glowing windows, imagining James returning to his vigil beside Richey's bed, imagining the quiet conversations he might have with his son in the darkness. She thought about the bottles poured down the drain, the windows opened to fresh air, the house being transformed into a home.

Small changes that might add up to something bigger. Something like hope.

Behind them, the hospital stood sentinel against the night sky, its windows like stars—each one containing stories of endings and beginnings, of breakings and healings. And somewhere inside, a heart continued to beat, monitored and measured, each pulse a tiny victory in the battle to return.

Sunday

Morning Light

Mariana woke before her alarm, pulled from sleep by the weight of consciousness rather than any external sound. Sunday morning light filtered through her curtains, casting soft patterns across her ceiling— the same ceiling she'd stared at for years, but which now seemed to belong to a different life entirely. Her body felt heavy, limbs leaden with the residual exhaustion that follows emotional storms.

She lay still, watching dust motes dance in the sunbeam crossing her room, and let the reality of the past forty-eight hours settle over her like sediment in still water.

Friday: the swim meet, the triumph, the party, the connection with Richey, then chaos. Saturday: the hospital, the machines, the police, James Vance's tears.

And now Sunday. The world still turning, indifferent to the fact that everything had changed.

Mariana turned onto her side, curling her knees toward her chest in a position that felt protective, though she wasn't sure what she was protecting herself from. Perhaps the inevitability of the day ahead— church, then the hospital, then Monday looming beyond that with all its complications.

School tomorrow. The thought alone made her stomach clench. By now, everyone would know. The rumor mill at Memorial High operated with ruthless efficiency. What version of Friday night had spread through social media and weekend gatherings? Was she the victim? The cause? The girl whose party mistake had cost the second-string quarterback his future?

She closed her eyes, trying to remember Richey as he had been in that quiet upstairs room at Jackie's house. The way he'd listened. The gentleness in his voice when he talked about feeling invisible. The moment their fingers had intertwined, natural as breathing.

Then she remembered him as she'd seen him yesterday—swollen, broken, silent beneath a tangle of tubes and wires. Barely recognizable as the boy who had kissed her just two nights ago.

"Stop," she whispered to herself. "This isn't helping."

She sat up, pushing hair from her face. Her room was exactly as she'd left it Friday morning—swim bag still packed for the meet, books stacked neatly on her desk, clothes for the party laid out then discarded. Evidence of a girl who had planned everything meticulously, never imagining how quickly plans could unravel.

A soft knock at her door pulled her from her thoughts.

"Come in," she called, her voice still rough with sleep.

Vanessa peeked in, already dressed in jeans and a green sweater, hair damp from the shower.

"Hey," she said. "You're up."

"Kind of," Mariana replied, shifting to make room as Vanessa entered and sat on the edge of the bed.

"Mom said you got home late from the hospital," Vanessa said, studying her sister's face. "How was it?"

Mariana pulled her knees to her chest. "Awful. Great. I don't know. Both, I guess."

"That makes no sense."

"None of this makes sense."

Vanessa nodded slowly. "Is he... is Richey going to be okay?"

Mariana looked down at her hands. "They don't know yet. He's in a coma—medically induced, to help with brain swelling. The doctor seemed cautiously optimistic, but..." She trailed off.

"But you're worried," Vanessa finished.

"Yeah."

They sat in silence for a moment, the weight of the situation settling between them. Then Vanessa nudged Mariana's foot.

"You know,' she said with a gentle smile, 'when I pictured your sweet sixteen celebration, I was thinking cake and presents—not hospital visits and police interviews. Leave it to you to go for maximum drama. "

Mariana snorted. "Shut up."

"Make me."

The familiar banter felt surreal in the context of everything that had happened, but also oddly comforting—a small island of normalcy in a sea of chaos.

"Have you checked your phone?" Vanessa asked, her tone shifting to something more serious.

Mariana glanced at her nightstand, where her phone lay face down, untouched since last night. "No. Why?"

"Just... prepare yourself. Everyone's talking about it."

"Great," Mariana groaned, falling back against her pillows. "What are they saying?"

Vanessa hesitated. "Different things. Some people think you and Richey were... you know. Others are saying Jackie went crazy for no reason. A few are saying Richey was drunk driving."

"He wasn't drunk," Mariana said firmly. "The police said his levels were low—barely anything."

"I'm just telling you what people are saying," Vanessa said gently. "It doesn't matter if it's true."

But it did matter. It mattered desperately. Mariana stared at the ceiling again, trying to organize her thoughts.

"I really liked him," she said suddenly, the words escaping before she could filter them. "Richey. I know that sounds crazy, since we barely talked before Friday, but when we did... it felt real. Like we'd known each other forever."

Vanessa didn't laugh or tease, which Mariana appreciated more than she could express.

"It's not crazy," Vanessa said. "Sometimes you just connect with someone. Like, instantly."

"And now he might..." Mariana couldn't bring herself to finish the thought.

"Don't," Vanessa said firmly. "Don't go there. He's going to be okay."

"You don't know that."

"No, but I'm choosing to believe it anyway," Vanessa replied. "And so should you."

Mariana turned to look at her sister—really look at her. At fourteen, Vanessa was already developing an emotional wisdom that sometimes surprised her. Beneath the teasing and the typical sister rivalry, there was a core of strength Mariana envied.

"How are you so good at this?" she asked.

Vanessa shrugged. "I've had a good role model. Even if she's being a total mess right now."

Mariana threw a pillow at her, and Vanessa caught it, laughing.

"Thanks," Mariana said. "For checking on me."

"That's what sisters do," Vanessa replied simply. "Besides, Dad's been asking about you all morning."

Mariana tensed. "He has?"

"Yeah. Mom told him most of it last night, but I think he wants to hear it from you." Vanessa stood. "He's making pancakes. The guilt kind with chocolate chips."

"Great."

"Hey," Vanessa said, pausing at the door. "It's going to be fine. Dad loves you. He's worried, not mad."

"I know."

After Vanessa left, Mariana forced herself out of bed. She knew she should look at her phone, deal with whatever messages were waiting, but she couldn't face that yet. Instead, she showered quickly, letting the hot water wash away the hospital smell that seemed to cling to her skin and hair.

Her church clothes hung ready in the closet—a modest blue dress with short sleeves, a cardigan to cover her shoulders in the sanctuary. She dressed mechanically, her mind already downstairs with the conversation waiting to happen.

When she finally made her way to the kitchen, the smell of coffee and pancakes wrapped around her like a familiar embrace. Her father stood at the stove, flipping a perfectly golden disk. He was a solid man, not tall but broad-shouldered, with the weathered hands of someone who had spent decades in physical labor. His face, so often serious, broke into a smile when he saw her.

"Mariana," he said, setting down his spatula. "*Buenos días, mi'ja.*"

"Morning, Dad."

Her mother sat at the table, coffee cup in hand, watching this exchange with careful eyes. Vanessa was setting the table, moving with deliberate noise as if to fill the awkward silence.

Her father gestured to the stack of pancakes. "Hungry?"

"A little," Mariana admitted, though her stomach felt twisted with anxiety.

They settled around the table, the routine of Sunday breakfast continuing despite the unspoken tension. Mariana accepted the plate her father pushed toward her, the chocolate chips in the pancakes forming a haphazard smiley face. It was something he'd done since she was small—pancake art that made her laugh even on difficult mornings.

Today, the gesture brought a lump to her throat.

"Your mother told me what happened," her father said finally, his accent thickening as it always did during serious conversations. "About the party. About the boy."

Mariana nodded, unable to meet his eyes. "I'm sorry, Dad."

"For what?" he asked, and the question surprised her enough to look up. His expression wasn't angry—it was concerned, tired, and something else she couldn't quite read. "For the lie about the party?

Yes, be sorry for that. But for trying to help this boy? For being there for him in the hospital? No. Don't be sorry for compassion."

Mariana blinked, thrown off balance by this unexpected response.

"I thought you'd be furious," she admitted.

Her father sighed heavily. "I was, at first. When your mother told me you had lied about where you were going, what you were doing..." He shook his head. "But then she told me about the accident. About the boy's father. About how you sat with them."

He cut a piece of pancake, his movements methodical. "Life is complicated, Mariana. People make mistakes. What matters is what you do after."

Gloria reached across the table, squeezing Mariana's hand. "Your father and I have talked a lot about this. About finding the balance between protecting you and... letting you learn."

"We came to this country so you could have more opportunities," her father continued. "Not just for school, for jobs. But to become the person God meant you to be." He looked at her intently. "Sometimes that person is made through difficult things."

Mariana felt tears threatening. "I've made such a mess of everything."

"No," her father said firmly. "You made one bad decision—lying about the party. But you've made many good ones since. Being honest with us. Going to the hospital. Supporting this boy and his father."

"Ricardo," Gloria interrupted gently, giving her husband a significant look. "There are still consequences for the lie."

He nodded. "Of course. No social activities for two weeks except school and swimming. And we need to know where you are, always." He paused. "But the hospital visits can continue. That boy needs all the support he can get."

Relief and gratitude washed over Mariana. "Thank you."

"This boy," her father said carefully. "Richey. You care about him?"

Mariana hesitated, then nodded. "Yes. I do."

Ricardo studied his daughter's face. "And his father? What kind of man is he?"

This was the question Mariana had been dreading. Her parents had always been careful about the company their daughters kept, always concerned about influences and backgrounds. James Vance—alcoholic, absent, struggling—wouldn't meet their usual standards.

"He's..." Mariana searched for the right words. "He's trying. Really trying. He poured out all his alcohol yesterday. Cleaned their house. He sits with Richey for hours, talking to him even though he can't respond."

Her parents exchanged glances, an entire conversation happening in that look.

"People can change," Ricardo said finally. "If they want to badly enough."

"Does he want to?" Gloria asked.

Mariana thought about James's breakdown in the hospital room, the raw honesty in his confession, the desperate hope in his voice when he talked about making a home for Richey's return.

"Yes," she said with certainty. "He does."

Ricardo nodded, seemingly satisfied. "Then we will help where we can." He checked his watch. "But now we must hurry, or we'll be late for Mass."

As they cleared the table, Mariana's phone buzzed in her pocket—a text. She pulled it out tentatively.

Daniel: Any updates? Going to visit this afternoon.

Relief flooded through her—just Daniel checking in, not some social media drama. She quickly replied:

Mariana: No change yet. We're going to Mass then the hospital. See you there?

Daniel: Yeah. Around 2. Bringing some of the guys from the team.

Mariana smiled faintly. Even in this mess, small kindnesses were emerging—her father's understanding, Daniel's steadfastness, the team's support. Perhaps there was a path through this after all.

As they prepared to leave for church, Mariana caught her reflection in the hallway mirror. She looked different somehow—older, certainly tired, but also steadier. As if the ground beneath her had shifted, but she had found her balance anyway.

"Ready?" her mother asked, handing Mariana her purse.

"Ready," she answered, and stepped outside into the clear Sunday morning light.

Sacred Spaces

The interior of St. Cyril of Alexandria Church was a sanctuary of light and shadow, the midday sun streaming through stained glass windows and casting jewel-toned patterns across the worn wooden pews. Mariana sat between her mother and Vanessa, the familiar weight of the hymnal in her hands, the melodic cadence of Spanish prayers washing over her like gentle waves.

Father Mario stood at the altar in green vestments, his voice resonant as he led the congregation through the liturgy. Mariana had known him since she was ten—he had given her First Communion, heard her stumbling confession in halting Spanish when she was nervous, celebrated her Quinceañera just last year. His familiar presence had always been a constant in her life, a spiritual anchor in the shifting tides of adolescence.

Today, though, she found it hard to focus on his homily. Her thoughts kept drifting to Room 214 at Memorial County Hospital, to the steady beep of monitors and the still form beneath hospital blankets. To James Vance, keeping his solitary vigil through the night. Had Richey's condition changed? Would today bring news—good or devastating?

"...y así, hermanos y hermanas, Dios nos llama a la compasión," Father Mario was saying. "God calls us to compassion, even—perhaps especially—when someone has made mistakes. Like the father in

181

today's Gospel, who runs to embrace his prodigal son..."

Mariana's attention sharpened. The priest's words suddenly seemed directed specifically at her situation.

"It is easy to love those who have done everything right," he continued, switching to English as he often did for emphasis. "Much harder to open our hearts to those who have stumbled. But that is precisely what Christ asks of us."

Beside her, Gloria reached over and squeezed Mariana's hand, as if sensing the relevance of these words to her daughter's current struggles. Mariana squeezed back, grateful for the silent support.

The Mass continued its ancient rhythm—the prayers, the responses, the ritual that had remained essentially unchanged for centuries. Mariana found comfort in this continuity, this sense that millions of others throughout time and space had voiced these same words, sought solace in these same rituals.

When it came time for Communion, she followed her family to the front of the church, hands folded, steps measured. Father Mario smiled kindly as he placed the host in her palm.

"*El Cuerpo de Cristo,*" he said.

"*Amén,*" she responded automatically.

As she returned to her seat and knelt in prayer, Mariana closed her eyes, trying to formulate the complicated feelings in her heart into something resembling a coherent prayer.

Please help Richey heal. Please give his father strength. Please help me understand what I'm supposed to learn from all this.

The simplicity of these requests felt right—direct, unadorned, honest in a way her prayers hadn't been for some time. She had grown accustomed to treating God like a cosmic vending machine: good grades in exchange for novenas, swimming victories in return for Mass attendance. Now, faced with something far beyond her control, she found herself stripping away the transactional nature of those prayers, reaching instead for something more authentic.

I don't know why this happened, she continued silently. *I don't know what comes next. But please don't let him die. Please don't let that be how this story ends.*

The final hymn began, voices rising in harmony around her. Mariana sang along, the familiar Spanish words flowing automatically, while her mind remained divided between the sacred space she occupied now and the sterile room she would visit later.

As the congregation filed out after the final blessing, Mariana paused near the side altar where dozens of votive candles flickered in red glass containers. This was where parishioners lit candles for special intentions—for sick relatives, for troubled children, for special needs of all kinds.

Without hesitation, she dropped a few dollars in the donation box, took a thin taper, and carefully lit a fresh candle. She placed it among the others, watching the small flame dance and settle.

For Richey, she thought. *For healing and strength.*

She stood there a moment longer, mesmerized by the collective glow of so many individual prayers burning together. There was something powerful in that image—separate intentions joining to create a greater light.

"That's a beautiful thing you're doing."

Mariana turned to find Mrs. Alvarez, one of her mother's friends from the parish council, standing beside her. The older woman's face was creased with smile lines, her eyes kind behind wire-rimmed glasses.

"Your mother told me about the boy," Mrs. Alvarez continued. "About the accident. I've added him to our prayer chain."

"Thank you," Mariana said, genuinely touched.

Mrs. Alvarez patted her arm. "God works in mysterious ways, *mija*. Sometimes the hardest moments are when His presence is most powerful."

As the woman moved away, Mariana considered her words. She wasn't sure if God had orchestrated this situation—the very idea that a divine plan might include Richey's suffering seemed cruel. But perhaps God was present in the response to tragedy: in James pouring out his alcohol, in Daniel rallying the team to visit, in her own parents extending compassion rather than judgment.

Perhaps God was in the small flames before her, each one a human heart reaching out in hope.

She rejoined her family in the vestibule, where her parents were chatting with several other couples. Her father had his "after-church" face on—serious but relaxed, engaging in the community gossip and news that always flowed freely between services.

"There you are," Gloria said, drawing Mariana into their circle. "We were just talking about where to have lunch before visiting the hospital."

Several of the adults exchanged glances at the mention of the hospital. Mariana could read the curiosity in their expressions, the questions they were too polite to ask directly.

Mrs. Reyes, a round-faced woman with immaculate makeup even at church, leaned in slightly. "How is the young man doing?" she asked in accented English.

"Stable," Gloria answered before Mariana could. "The doctors are cautiously optimistic."

"Such a terrible thing," Mr. Diaz commented, shaking his head. "Sixteen years old. A reminder of how fragile life is, no?"

Mariana felt a flash of irritation at having Richey reduced to a moral lesson, a cautionary tale for other teenagers. He was more than that— more than the accident, more than his mistakes.

"He's a good person," she said, more firmly than she'd intended. "He plays football. He's smart. He takes care of his father. And he—" She stopped, suddenly conscious of all the adults studying her with varying degrees of surprise.

Her father placed a steadying hand on her shoulder. "We should get going," he said, smoothly changing the subject. "We promised to be at the hospital by one."

As they said their goodbyes and moved toward the parking lot,

Vanessa nudged Mariana gently.

"Way to defend your boyfriend," she whispered.

"He's not my boyfriend," Mariana replied automatically, though the denial felt hollow even to her own ears.

Vanessa raised an eyebrow but said nothing more, sliding into the backseat of their SUV beside Mariana.

The drive to Los Cucos, their usual Sunday lunch spot, was quiet, each family member absorbed in their own thoughts. Mariana watched the familiar Houston landscape slide past—strip malls, apartment complexes, palm trees swaying in the gentle breeze. The ordinary world continuing, oblivious to how drastically her inner landscape had changed in just two days.

The restaurant was crowded with after-church families, the air thick with the scent of sizzling fajitas and fresh tortillas. They were shown to their usual corner booth, the waiter already knowing to bring Ricardo his horchata and Gloria her iced tea with extra lemon.

As they settled in, Gloria studied the menu she already knew by heart. "Perhaps we should bring something for Mr. Vance," she suggested. "Hospital food isn't very satisfying."

Mariana looked up, surprised by this thoughtfulness. "That would be nice."

"What does he like?" Ricardo asked, setting down his menu.

Mariana realized she had no idea. In the intensity of their shared crisis, such basic information about James Vance had never come up. "I'm not sure," she admitted. "But anything would probably be welcome."

"We'll order an extra plate of enchiladas," Gloria decided. "Every man appreciates a good meal in difficult times."

The casual inclusion of James in their plans touched Mariana deeply. Her parents, who had always been so careful about the company their daughters kept, were extending grace to a man they had every reason to distrust. It spoke volumes about their character— and gave Mariana a renewed appreciation for the values they had tried to instill in her.

As they waited for their food, Ricardo leaned forward, his expression turning more serious. "Mariana, your mother and I have been talking. About tomorrow."

Mariana tensed. Monday. School. The return to normal life that would be anything but normal.

"What about it?" she asked cautiously.

"We think perhaps you should stay home," he said. "Just for a day or two, until things settle."

Mariana blinked in surprise. Her parents had always been strict about school attendance—a missed day required either a significant fever or a doctor's note.

"The guidance counselor called this morning," Gloria explained. "There's been a lot of talk among students. About the party. About Richey. About you."

"What kind of talk?" Mariana asked, though she could imagine.

Her parents exchanged glances. "Nothing you need to worry about now," her father said firmly. "But we thought you might appreciate a little space. Time to process everything before facing questions."

Mariana considered this. Part of her wanted to hide, to avoid the whispers and stares that would inevitably follow her through the hallways. But another part recognized that delaying would only make the eventual return more difficult.

"I appreciate that," she said slowly. "But I think I need to go. Face whatever's waiting. The longer I stay away, the worse the rumors will get."

Her father studied her face, then nodded with something like pride. "If that's what you want."

"It's not what I want," Mariana admitted. "But I think it's what I need to do."

As their food arrived, steaming and aromatic, Vanessa changed the subject to her upcoming volleyball tryouts, and conversation shifted to lighter topics. Mariana ate mechanically, her thoughts already at the hospital. What would they find when they arrived? Would there be any improvement? Would the football team be there, as Daniel had mentioned?

And what about James—had he managed any rest, or had he spent the entire night in that uncomfortable chair, watching his son's chest rise and fall to the rhythm of machines?

By the time they finished lunch, it was nearly one-thirty. As they drove toward Memorial County Hospital, Mariana felt the familiar tension return to her shoulders, the mixture of hope and dread that seemed to define this new reality.

The hospital parking lot was more crowded than it had been yesterday—Sunday visitors filling spaces that had been empty on Saturday. They circled twice before finding a spot near the back, the to-go container of enchiladas carefully balanced on Mariana's lap.

As they approached the main entrance, Mariana spotted a cluster of familiar figures—tall, broad-shouldered young men in Memorial High letter jackets. The football team, or at least part of it. Daniel stood among them, his track runner's build leaner than most of his football teammates, but his presence just as meaningful—the receiver who caught Richey's passes, the friend who'd been there since elementary school.

"Mariana!" he called, catching sight of her. "We were just heading in."

She quickened her pace, her family following. "Hey," she said, reaching the group. "I didn't know there would be so many of you."

Chad stepped forward, his imposing frame making even her father look small by comparison. "We wanted to show support," he said, his usual bravado subdued. "Coach Kenneck would have come, but he's dealing with reporters. They've been calling all weekend."

Mariana hadn't considered that aspect—that Richey's accident would be newsworthy beyond their immediate circle. But of course it would be. The starting quarterback hospitalized before a crucial game, the championship hopes of Memorial High suddenly in jeopardy.

"Any update?" Daniel asked as they all moved toward the entrance.

Mariana shook her head. "Not since last night. His dad's been here the whole time."

Inside, the hospital lobby was bustling with Sunday visitors. The football players drew attention—their size, their letter jackets, their collective presence creating a ripple of curious glances. They made their way to the elevators, a strange procession of teenage athletes, the Garcia family, and the solitary container of enchiladas.

"ICU might have restrictions on visitors," Gloria cautioned as they rode upward. "They may not let everyone in at once."

Chad nodded. "We figured. We can take turns."

When they reached the ICU floor, a nurse at the station looked up with alarm at the sudden influx of visitors. "Can I help you?" she asked, her tone making it clear that a dozen people couldn't descend on her ward simultaneously.

"We're here to see Richey Vance," Daniel explained. "Room 214. We know we can't all go in at once."

The nurse's expression softened slightly. "Are you all... friends?"

"Teammates," Chad said. "From Memorial High. We just wanted to show our support."

The nurse assessed the group, then nodded. "Two at a time, please. Five minutes each pair. And keep it quiet—this is an intensive care unit, not a pep rally."

As the group sorted out who would go first, Mariana approached the desk. "Is his father still here? Mr. Vance?"

"Hasn't left," the nurse confirmed. "Well, except to shower this morning. He's been a fixture in that room since admission."

Mariana felt a surge of both admiration and concern for James. "We brought him food," she said, raising the container slightly.

"That was thoughtful," the nurse said, her professional demeanor warming further. "You can take it in."

Chad and another senior linebacker went in first, their massive frames suddenly awkward and hesitant as they entered the quiet realm of the ICU.

Inside the room, Chad stopped short, the confident swagger vanishing at the sight of Richey connected to so many machines. He'd gotten the text from Coach Kenneck that morning: "Richey Vance has been in a serious accident. In ICU. More details when we have them. Team meeting Monday morning."

He'd stared at his phone for a long time, unexpected emotions churning through him. Just 2 days ago at practice, he'd seen something in Richey—something he recognized and respected. A hunger that matched his own.

"Damn," he whispered, approaching the bed.

The other linebacker hung back near the door, clearly uncomfortable.

"Hey, Broke," Chad said softly. "This isn't what I meant when I said I'd flatten you." He attempted a smile that didn't quite reach his eyes.

He shifted his weight, looking around at the machines as if searching for something familiar. "The team's behind you. One hundred percent." He cleared his throat. "You were supposed to prove me wrong on the field, man. And you still will."

After a few minutes, they emerged, faces somber, making way for the next pair.

Mariana watched this rotation, observing each pair of teammates as they returned from Room 214. Some looked shaken, others determined, a few fighting back tears. These boys—many of whom she knew only as distant figures at pep rallies or faces in the hallway— were showing a depth of loyalty that moved her.

When Daniel emerged with Kyle, the last of the teammates to visit, he came directly to Mariana.

"He looks better than yesterday," he said quietly. "Less swollen. His dad says the pressure in his brain is down."

A wave of relief washed over Mariana. "Really?"

Daniel nodded. "They're talking about reducing the sedation tomorrow if the numbers keep improving. Maybe let him start waking up."

Mariana felt dizzy with hope. "That's—that's great news."

Daniel glanced at her family, then back to her. "His dad's been telling him about all the visitors. About you especially. I think it helps, having you here."

Before Mariana could respond, her father stepped forward. "We should go in," he said gently. "Before visiting hours end."

The football team began to disperse, each player stopping to shake Ricardo's hand or nod respectfully to Gloria before heading toward the elevators. Their quiet dignity in this situation—so contrary to their usual boisterous hallway presence—left a powerful impression.

As they approached Room 214, Mariana felt a now-familiar tightening in her chest. No matter how many times she entered this space, she didn't think she would ever get used to seeing Richey this way—vulnerable, silent, dependent on machines to perform the basic functions of life.

Her father held the door open, allowing Gloria and Vanessa to enter first, then Mariana.

Sacred Spaces part 2

Inside Room 214, the scene was much as it had been yesterday, yet subtly different. The same machines hummed and beeped, the same tubes and wires connected Richey to various forms of support. But James Vance sat straighter in his chair, his appearance markedly improved from the day before. He'd shaved, changed his clothes, and though exhaustion still shadowed his eyes, there was a clarity to his gaze that spoke of hard-won sobriety maintained through the night.

He stood when they entered, seeming momentarily overwhelmed by the sudden influx of visitors.

"Mr. and Mrs. Garcia," he said, his voice rough but steady. "Thank you for coming."

Ricardo stepped forward, extending his hand. "Ricardo Garcia," he said. "This is my wife, Gloria, and our younger daughter, Vanessa."

James shook hands with each of them, the formality of these introductions creating a strange counterpoint to the gravity of the situation.

"How is he?" Gloria asked, her gaze moving to Richey.

"Better," James said, turning back to his son. "The swelling in his brain has decreased consistently since early this morning. His oxygen levels are stronger. They've reduced one of the medications." He recited these improvements like treasured verses, each one a small victory in the battle for Richey's recovery.

Mariana moved to the bedside, studying Richey's face. Daniel was right—the swelling had visibly decreased, the bruising around his eyes now yellowing at the edges rather than the angry purple of yesterday. His breathing seemed deeper, more natural, despite the ventilator's continued assistance.

"We brought you something to eat," Gloria said, handing James the container. "Hospital food can be... difficult."

James looked momentarily stunned by this simple kindness. "Thank you," he said, accepting the container. "That's very thoughtful."

"It's nothing," Gloria replied. "Just enchiladas from Los Cucos."

"That's Richey's favorite place," James said, his voice catching slightly. "He loves their enchiladas suizas. Always has, since he was little."

The coincidence hung in the air between them, a small thread connecting these strangers whose lives had suddenly become intertwined.

Ricardo moved closer to the bed, studying Richey with the careful assessment of a father. "Strong boy," he commented. "You can see it in his build."

"Football and determination," James agreed. "Gets that from his mother. She never backed down from anything."

The mention of Richey's mother created a moment of hesitation. Mariana watched her parents exchange a quick glance, undoubtedly wondering about the absent woman but too polite to ask directly.

James seemed to sense their question. "She lives on the East Coast now. Remarried. I called her yesterday." He paused. "She's trying to get a flight down."

"That's good," Gloria said gently. "He'll need all his family."

James nodded, though his expression suggested complicated feelings about this reunion. He turned to Vanessa, who had been standing quietly near the door. "You're Mariana's sister?"

"Yes, sir," Vanessa replied. "I'm fourteen."

"Richey mentioned you too," James said, surprising everyone. "Said you're the only freshman who wasn't afraid to argue with seniors in the lunch line."

Vanessa blinked, then smiled cautiously. "They were cutting in front of everyone."

A ghost of a smile touched James's face. "He was impressed. Said you had 'serious backbone.'"

This small revelation—that Richey had noticed Vanessa, had spoken about her to his father—seemed to ease some of the tension in the room. They were no longer simply strangers brought together by tragedy, but people connected by the threads of ordinary school days, cafeteria encounters, shared Mexican restaurants.

"The football team seems very supportive," Gloria observed, gesturing toward the hallway where the last few players were departing.

"They're good kids," James said. "Better than I expected, to be honest. I haven't... I haven't been to many games." The admission clearly pained him. "An'other thing I got wrong."

Ricardo stepped forward. "Mr. Vance—"

"James, please."

"James," Ricardo amended. "May I speak plainly?"

James straightened, as if bracing himself. "Of course."

"My daughter tells me you've made changes. Important ones." Ricardo's voice was steady, neither accusing nor particularly warm. Just direct. "That matters. But what matters more is what happens when Richey wakes up. When the crisis passes."

James met Ricardo's gaze unflinchingly. "I know."

"Do you?" Ricardo pressed. "Because promises made in hospital rooms sometimes fade when life returns to normal."

"Ricardo," Gloria cautioned, but he continued.

"I say this not to judge, but because I've seen it before. In my own family. My uncle—a good man, a loving father—who would swear on his children's lives every time one of them was hurt or sick. Who meant it with his whole heart in those moments. But who could not maintain that commitment when the emergency passed."

The room fell silent except for the steady beep of the monitors. James didn't look away from Ricardo's intense gaze.

"I understand what you're saying," he said finally. "And I don't blame you for the warning. I haven't earned anyone's trust yet." He glanced at Richey. "Especially not his."

"But you want to," Ricardo said. It wasn't a question.

"More than anything." James's voice broke slightly. "I've wasted so many years. Missed so much. And now, seeing him like this..." He gestured helplessly at the bed. "What if this is all I get? What if I never get the chance to make it right?"

The naked vulnerability in his question cut through any remaining formality. Gloria stepped forward, placing a gentle hand on James's arm.

"He will wake up," she said firmly. "And then the real work begins. For both of you."

James nodded, unable to speak.

Ricardo's expression softened. "You're not alone in this, James. Whatever happens."

The simple declaration hung in the air, powerful in its unexpectedness. Mariana watched her father—always cautious, always protective of his family—extend a hand to this broken man he barely knew. It was a side of him she had glimpsed before, but rarely so openly displayed.

"Thank you," James managed.

A nurse appeared at the door. "I need to check his vitals," she said apologetically. "Could I ask most of you to step out for a few minutes?"

"Of course," Gloria replied. "Ricardo, Vanessa—let's get some coffee."

Ricardo glanced at Mariana. "You coming, *mija*?"

"Can I stay?" she asked, looking from the nurse to James.

The nurse nodded. "Just for a few minutes. I need to change some bandages."

As her family filed out, Mariana moved to stand beside James, both of them watching as the nurse efficiently checked monitors, recorded numbers, and examined the various tubes and connections.

"His color's better today," the nurse commented. "And his latest scan showed significant improvement in the cerebral edema."

"That's the brain swelling," James explained to Mariana, the medical terminology already familiar to him after countless conversations with doctors.

The nurse nodded approvingly. "Dr. Mehta will be by later to discuss next steps. But things are moving in the right direction."

After she left, a different quality of silence filled the room. James sat heavily in his chair, the weight of constant vigilance evident in every line of his body.

"Have you slept at all?" Mariana asked.

"A little. In the chair." He rubbed his face. "Went home early this morning to shower. Couldn't stay away long."

Mariana understood. The fear that something might change in your absence, that the one moment you stepped away might be the critical one.

"He looks better," she offered.

"Yeah." James reached out to adjust Richey's blanket, a small, automatic gesture of care. "They say hearing is the last sense to go, the first to return. So I've been talking to him. Probably driving him crazy."

"What do you talk about?"

James smiled faintly. "Everything. Nothing. Old memories. Things I should have said years ago." He glanced at her. "You."

Mariana felt her cheeks warm. "Me?"

"I tell him you've been here. That you're coming back." James hesitated. "I think it helps. When I mention you, sometimes his heart rate changes. Just a little."

The thought that Richey might be aware of her presence, even in some small way, sent a wave of emotion through Mariana's chest.

"Can I... would it be okay if I had a moment alone with him?" she asked hesitantly.

James nodded immediately, standing with a wince as stiff muscles protested. "Of course. I could use some air anyway." He paused at the door. "Take your time."

When the door closed behind him, Mariana moved closer to the bed. Now that they were alone, she felt suddenly unsure what to do, what to say. She gently took Richey's hand, careful of the IV line, and was struck by its warmth. Despite all the equipment, all the medical intervention, this was still him—still the boy who had made her feel seen just two nights ago.

"Hi," she said softly. "It's Mariana again."

The monitors continued their steady rhythm, giving no indication that he heard her.

"I don't know if you can hear me, but I wanted you to know that I'm thinking about you. All the time, actually." She smiled, though he couldn't see it. "I lit a candle for you at church today. And I've been praying, which is something I haven't done very seriously in a while."

She stroked the back of his hand with her thumb, finding comfort in the small connection.

"Your dad is trying so hard, Richey. I wish you could see it. He hasn't left your side except to shower. He's talking to my parents like they're old friends. And he hasn't been drinking—I can tell."

The words flowed more easily now, as if she were simply having a conversation with the Richey she had met at the party, the one who had listened so attentively.

"I have to go back to school tomorrow. I'm kind of terrified, to be honest. Everyone's talking, and I don't know what they're saying, but I know it's about us. About what happened." She sighed. "But that doesn't matter. None of it matters except you getting better."

She leaned closer, her voice dropping to a near-whisper. "I need you to wake up, Richey. I need you to come back. There's so much more I want to know about you. So much more I want to say."

On impulse, she leaned forward and pressed a gentle kiss to his forehead, careful to avoid the line of stitches. "Just keep fighting, okay? I'll be back tomorrow after school. I promise."

She stayed there a moment longer, her hand in his, memorizing the details of his face—not as it was now, bruised and swollen, but as it had been in those quiet moments at Jackie's house. The way his eyes crinkled slightly when he smiled. The small scar near his eyebrow that she'd noticed when they sat close together.

A soft knock at the door brought her back to the present. She quickly wiped her eyes, not having realized she'd been crying, and called, "Come in."

James entered, carrying two cups of coffee. He handed one to her. "Thought you might need this."

"Thank you." She accepted the cup gratefully, the warmth seeping into her hands.

They stood in companionable silence, each lost in their own thoughts, until the door opened again and Dr. Mehta entered, tablet in hand. Her expression was carefully professional, but there was a hint of something positive in her eyes.

"Mr. Vance," she greeted him, then nodded to Mariana. "I have the results from this afternoon's tests."

James stiffened, his hand tightening around his coffee cup. "And?"

"The intra-cranial pressure has decreased significantly. The latest EEG shows improved brain activity. His lungs are functioning better, though we'll keep him on ventilator support for now." She looked directly at James. "If these trends continue overnight, we'll begin reducing the sedation tomorrow morning."

The cup trembled in James's hand. "Reducing—you mean waking him up?"

"Gradually," Dr. Mehta cautioned. "It's not like in the movies. It's a process, not a moment. And we need to be prepared for various outcomes. But yes, we would begin the process of allowing him to regain consciousness."

James set his cup down carefully, as if afraid he might drop it.

"What are the risks?"

Dr. Mehta's expression remained measured. "There's always uncertainty with traumatic brain injuries. He might experience confusion, memory issues, changes in cognitive function or motor skills. We won't know the full extent until he's awake and we can assess him properly."

"But he'll be Richey," James pressed. "Himself."

"The core of who he is should remain," Dr. Mehta said, choosing her words with obvious care. "But there may be changes. We need to be prepared for that possibility."

James nodded, absorbing this. "When tomorrow?"

"I'll be here at eight to evaluate his overnight readings. If everything looks good, we'll begin reducing sedation around nine." She made a notation on her tablet. "I'd suggest you get some proper rest tonight, Mr. Vance. Tomorrow may be a long day."

After the doctor left, James sank into his chair, the mixture of hope and fear plain on his face.

"He's coming back," Mariana said, her voice breaking with emotion.

"Maybe," James replied, always the cautious one now. "If things keep improving."

"They will," Mariana insisted. She glanced at her watch reluctantly. "I should find my parents. It's getting late, and I have school tomorrow."

James nodded. "Of course." He hesitated, then added, "Thank you. For everything. For being here. For your parents." He gestured to the now-empty container of enchiladas. "For food that reminds me there's a world outside these walls."

"We'll be back," Mariana promised. "After school tomorrow."

"I'll call if anything changes," James said. "Anything at all."

As Mariana turned to leave, she took one last look at Richey—at the machines that had become so familiar in just two days, at the father who maintained his vigil with newfound determination. Then she slipped out the door, leaving the two of them alone.

The room grew quieter after Mariana left, the emotional current she brought with her receding like a tide, leaving James alone with his son and the steady rhythm of the machines. He leaned forward in his chair, taking Richey's hand gently in his.

"It's just us again, son," he said softly.

The words came easier now, after so many hours of one-sided conversation. He'd talked himself nearly hoarse yesterday, telling Richey stories from his childhood, confessing mistakes, making promises. Today, with the possibility of Richey actually waking tomorrow, his words felt more weighted, more purposeful.

"The doctor says they might start waking you up tomorrow," he continued. "So I need you to keep fighting. Keep healing. Whatever it takes."

He studied his son's face, searching for any sign of awareness. The bruising had changed colors, moving from deep purple to the sickly yellow-green of healing. The swelling had decreased enough that Richey was beginning to look more like himself again.

"Your mom called again," James said. "She's got a flight tomorrow morning. Should be here by afternoon." He paused. "I know things have been complicated between you two. But she loves you, Richey. Never doubt that."

The mention of Eleanor still caused a constriction in his chest—not the sharp pain of their early separation, but a duller ache of regret for what might have been. She'd tried. God knows, she'd tried to help him after Bobby died, to pull him back from the edge of his grief and rage. But he'd been too far gone, too determined to drown his guilt in bourbon and blame.

"I was so wrong," James continued, his voice dropping to a whisper. "About so many things. But especially about her. I told you she abandoned us, but that wasn't true. I pushed her away. Made it impossible for her to stay. Even those first couple of years after she left, when she still came for visits, I made it difficult."

He rubbed his thumb across Richey's knuckles, noting how the same gesture had seemed to comfort Mariana earlier.

"When you wake up, I want us to talk about her. About everything I've kept from you. No more lies. No more hiding behind the bottle." His voice grew fierce. "I'm fighting for you, son. And I'm fighting for me too. For what we could be."

James fell silent for a moment, watching the steady rise and fall of Richey's chest, the blinking lights on the monitors that had become a strange source of comfort over the past two days.

"The Garcia family is something else," he said eventually, his tone lighter. "Mr. Garcia gave me the third degree—politely, of course. Can't say I blame him. If our situations were reversed, I'd be suspicious too."

He smiled faintly, picturing Ricardo's intense gaze, Gloria's gentle diplomacy, Vanessa's careful assessment.

"And Mariana... she's special, Richey. Smart. Compassionate. Stronger than she looks." He chuckled softly. "She reminds me of your mother, actually. That same quiet determination. That way of seeing right through bullshit."

The monitor beeped, a slight fluctuation in heart rate that made James sit up straighter, watching intently. After a moment, the rhythm returned to normal, but James liked to think it was a response—some small indication that Richey heard him, especially when he talked about Mariana.

"I think she really cares about you," James continued. "The way she looks at you... it's not just guilt or pity. It's something real." He squeezed Richey's hand gently. "And when you wake up, you'll see that for yourself."

The night nurse appeared in the doorway, clipboard in hand. "Time for the evening check," she said apologetically.

James nodded, releasing Richey's hand and standing to give her space. He moved to the window, staring out at the hospital campus below, lit by security lights against the gathering dusk. Sunday evening. In another life—the life of just three days ago—he might have been on the couch by now, halfway through a six-pack, television blaring to drown out his thoughts.

Tonight, he was clearheaded. Present. Terrified and hopeful in equal measure.

The nurse completed her checks, making notations on her clipboard. "Everything looks stable," she reported. "Dr. Mehta left orders for hourly monitoring overnight, in preparation for tomorrow."

"Thank you," James said. "I appreciate everything you're all doing."

She smiled—the first genuine smile he'd received from the nursing staff. "You're doing the hard part, Mr. Vance. Just being here. It matters."

After she left, James returned to his chair, feeling the fatigue of constant vigilance settle deeper into his bones. Dr. Mehta had suggested he get proper rest tonight, but the thought of leaving—of not being here if Richey showed any sign of waking—was unthinkable.

"Just you and me, kid," he murmured, settling in. "One more night. And then tomorrow... tomorrow we start again."

Outside, night fell fully over Houston, stars emerging in the clear sky. Inside Room 214, a father kept watch, sustained by enchiladas and coffee, by small medical improvements, by the possibility of redemption. And through the long hours of the night, the machines continued their vigil alongside him, marking each heartbeat, each breath, each precious moment of his son's continued presence in the world.

As the hospital quieted around him, James found himself drifting between wakefulness and memory. He studied Richey's face, so still beneath the ventilator tube, and suddenly remembered another night of watchfulness, years ago.

Richey had been six, burning with fever, small body shivering despite the blankets piled on his twin bed. The pediatrician had said it was just a virus—keep him hydrated, monitor his temperature, call if it spiked above 103. Eleanor had finally fallen asleep in their bedroom after two sleepless nights.

"I'll take this shift," James had whispered, kissing her forehead. "Get some rest."

He'd sat beside Richey's bed all night, applying cool washcloths to his forehead, checking the digital thermometer hourly, feeling utterly helpless against the invisible enemy attacking his son.

"Dad?" Richey had whispered sometime in the darkest hours, his eyes glassy with fever.

"I'm here, buddy."

"Don't go, okay?"

"I'm not going anywhere," James had promised, taking his son's small, hot hand in his own. "Not until you're better."

Richey had drifted back to sleep, his breathing gradually steadying, his hand still wrapped in his father's.

By morning, the fever had broken. The crisis had passed. And James had felt something he couldn't articulate—a fierce pride that had nothing to do with achievement and everything to do with simply being there, being the father his son needed.

What had happened to that father? When had he started breaking those simple, essential promises?

James rubbed his eyes, the memory both comfort and accusation. He looked at the monitors, at their steady rhythm marking his son's precarious hold on life. This time would be different. This time, when Richey opened his eyes—if he opened his eyes—James would still be there, just as he'd promised all those years ago.

"I'm not going anywhere," he whispered again, the words both echo and pledge. "Not this time."

Monday

Empty Spaces

Monday morning announced itself with the harsh buzz of Mariana's alarm clock. She reached out automatically to silence it, then lay still, eyes fixed on the ceiling, reality settling over her like a heavy blanket. The weekend's events replayed in rapid succession—the party, the accident, the hospital. And now, somehow, she was expected to return to normal life, to classrooms and homework and swim practice.

She sat up slowly, checking her phone. No missed calls, which meant no emergency updates about Richey overnight. That was good. She scrolled through a barrage of notifications—messages from teammates, from classmates, even from people she barely knew, all asking variations of the same questions.

Is it true? What happened? Are you okay?

She ignored them all, thumb hovering briefly over Jackie's name among the unread texts before swiping away. She wasn't ready for that conversation yet.

As she slid out of bed, her phone buzzed with a new message. Her heart jumped, thinking it might be James with news, but it was Jackie again.

Jackie: Can we please talk before class? I'll be at the north entrance at 7:30. Please, Mari.

Mariana stared at the message, conflicting emotions churning in her stomach. Part of her wanted to ignore Jackie completely, to punish her for the cascade of events her drunken accusations had triggered. But another part recognized the futility of avoidance. They shared too many classes, too many friends. Better to face it head-on than dodge around the edges.

Mariana: Ok. 7:30.

The response was immediate.

Jackie: Thank you. Really.

Mariana set her phone down and moved to her closet. What did you wear to face a school full of rumors about yourself? Everything in her wardrobe suddenly seemed too bright or too somber, too attention-seeking or too much like hiding.

She settled on jeans and a simple blue sweater—ordinary, unremarkable, a uniform of normalcy. As she dressed, she tried to prepare herself mentally for the day ahead. The stares. The whispers. The questions she had no interest in answering.

The bathroom was mercifully empty, Vanessa apparently still asleep. Mariana brushed her teeth and washed her face, studying her reflection critically. She looked tired, the shadows under her eyes betraying her restless night. She applied a little concealer, some mascara, a touch of lip gloss—armor of a different kind.

Downstairs, she found her mother at the kitchen counter, packing lunch for Vanessa.

"Morning," Gloria said, looking up with careful assessment. "Sleep okay?"

"Not really," Mariana admitted, reaching for a banana from the fruit bowl.

"You don't have to go today," her mother reminded her. "Dad and I meant what we said."

Mariana shook her head. "Better to get it over with."

Gloria nodded, understanding without needing further explanation. "I put your lunch in your backpack. And I called Coach Riley. Told him you might skip practice today."

"Mom, I can still—"

"It's not required," Gloria interrupted gently. "Just for today. Give yourself a break."

Mariana wanted to argue but found she didn't have the energy. Maybe her mother was right. Maybe she did need a break—just this once.

"Thanks," she said instead, peeling her banana without much appetite.

Gloria stopped what she was doing and moved to place her hands on Mariana's shoulders. "Listen to me. Whatever happens today, whatever people say—you know the truth. That's what matters."

Mariana nodded, unable to speak past the sudden tightness in her throat.

"And if it gets to be too much, call me. I'll come get you."

"I'll be fine, Mom."

"I know you will," Gloria said, her eyes reflecting both pride and concern. "You're stronger than you think."

Ricardo appeared in the doorway, car keys already in hand. "Ready to go, *mija*?"

Mariana nodded, shouldering her backpack. Her father usually left earlier for work, but today he had rearranged his schedule to drive her to school himself. Another small kindness she hadn't expected but deeply appreciated.

The drive was quiet, the morning traffic already building as they made their way toward Memorial High. Mariana watched the familiar landmarks pass, each one bringing her closer to a day she was dreading.

"You know," her father said, breaking the silence, "when I first came to this country, people stared at me too. Whispered. Made assumptions."

Mariana turned to look at him, surprised by this rare glimpse into his past.

"I couldn't speak much English," he continued. "Worked construction with mostly other immigrants. The foreman would yell instructions I barely understood. The American workers would laugh when I made mistakes." He glanced at her. "It was... difficult."

"What did you do?" Mariana asked.

Ricardo smiled slightly. "I held my head high. Did my work. Learned English at night classes. And eventually, I became the foreman."

The message behind the story wasn't subtle, but it resonated nonetheless. Dignity. Perseverance. The long view.

"Thanks, Dad," Mariana said softly.

As they approached the school, Mariana's stomach tightened. The familiar redbrick building, the flagpole, the buses disgorging sleepy students—it all looked so normal. But for her, everything had changed.

Ricardo pulled into the drop-off lane, putting the car in park. "You call if you need anything. Anything at all."

"I will."

"And Mariana?" She paused with her hand on the door handle. "We're proud of you. For facing this. For standing by Richey and his father. That takes courage."

His words gave her strength, a warmth that spread through her chest. "Love you, Dad."

"Love you too, *mi'ja*."

Mariana stepped out of the car, taking a deep breath of the cool morning air. Students streamed toward the entrance, backpacks slung over shoulders, faces still puffy with sleep, the usual Monday morning energy—part reluctance, part resignation.

She made her way toward the north entrance where Jackie would be waiting. As she crossed the faculty parking lot, she became aware of the attention she was drawing. Conversations paused as she passed. Heads turned. Eyes followed her progress. Some gazes were merely curious, others more pointed. A few people smiled tentatively or nodded, but most quickly looked away when she made eye contact.

So this was what it felt like to become part of the school's mythology overnight. To transform from just another student into The Girl From

The Accident. The center of gossip and speculation.

She kept her chin up, her pace steady, Ricardo's words echoing in her mind. *Hold your head high. The long view.*

Jackie was waiting as promised, standing nervously by the side entrance, chewing on her lower lip. When she spotted Mariana, her expression cycled rapidly through anxiety, relief, and fear.

"Hey," Jackie said as Mariana approached, her voice smaller than usual. "Thanks for coming."

Mariana nodded, not trusting herself to speak yet. Up close, Jackie looked as exhausted as Mariana felt, her usual perfect appearance slightly frayed at the edges.

"Can we..." Jackie glanced around at the students moving past them, many openly staring now. "Can we go somewhere a little more private?"

They found a relatively quiet corner near the art classrooms, which wouldn't fill up until later periods. Jackie leaned against the wall, fidgeting with the strap of her designer handbag.

"How is he?" she asked, cutting straight to the question that mattered most.

"Still in the ICU," Mariana replied. "But they might start reducing the sedation today. Maybe let him wake up if his brain swelling keeps improving."

Relief washed over Jackie's face. "That's good, right? That means he'll be okay?"

"They don't know yet. There could be... lasting effects." Mariana struggled to keep her voice steady. "They won't know until he's awake."

Jackie nodded, absorbing this. "I am so, so sorry, Mariana. I never meant—" She broke off, blinking rapidly. "I was drunk and stupid and jumped to conclusions. And now he's in the hospital and everyone's talking and it's all my fault."

The naked guilt in Jackie's voice defused some of Mariana's anger. Not all of it—part of her still burned with resentment for the chaos

Jackie's accusations had unleashed—but enough to soften her response.

"It wasn't just you," Mariana said finally. "It was a lot of things. The party without supervision. The alcohol. Richey feeling like no one would believe him." She sighed. "No one person caused this."

"But I made it so much worse," Jackie insisted. "If I hadn't started screaming like that—"

"You can't change what happened," Mariana interrupted. "None of us can. All we can do now is deal with what is."

Jackie studied her face. "You really care about him, don't you? It wasn't just a one-night party thing."

Mariana hesitated, then nodded. "Yeah. I do."

"I didn't know," Jackie said softly. "I mean, I knew you guys were talking, but I didn't realize it was... serious."

"I don't know what it is," Mariana admitted. "Or what it might have been. But it felt real."

They stood in silence for a moment, the background noise of students arriving for the day washing over them. The first warning bell would ring soon, pushing them into the rhythms of the school day whether they were ready or not.

"What can I do?" Jackie asked finally. "To help. To make up for—for everything."

Mariana considered this. "Stop the rumors. If you hear people talking, tell them what really happened. That Richey didn't do anything wrong."

Jackie nodded quickly. "I've already been trying. I posted on Instagram last night. Told everyone I'd overreacted, that nothing had happened."

"Thank you."

"And—I want to come to the hospital. To apologize to him properly. When he wakes up."

Mariana wasn't sure how to respond to that. The thought of Jackie in Richey's hospital room, explaining her drunken accusations to a boy who might still be struggling with the physical aftermath of his injuries, seemed potentially harmful rather than healing.

"Let's wait on that," she said diplomatically. "See how he is first."

Jackie looked disappointed but nodded. "Whatever you think is best."

The first bell rang, its sharp electronic tone cutting through their conversation. Students quickened their pace, lockers slammed, the hallway energy shifting into pre-class chaos.

"We should go," Mariana said, already dreading the classroom gauntlet ahead.

"Can I walk with you?" Jackie asked hesitantly. "To homeroom?"

The request surprised Mariana. It was both a peace offering and a public statement—Jackie aligning herself with Mariana despite the rumors, making her position clear.

"Okay," Mariana agreed.

As they moved through the now-crowded hallway, Mariana spotted Daniel by his locker, his head bent in conversation with Chad. Daniel looked up, catching her eye, and broke away to intercept them.

"Hey," he said, his usual easygoing manner subdued. "Any news?"

"They might start waking him up today," Mariana reported. "If the brain swelling continues to improve."

Relief crossed Daniel's face. "That's good. Really good." He paused, glancing at Jackie with barely disguised coolness before turning back to Mariana. "I'm heading over there after school. My mom wants to meet his dad. Bring some things for his hospital room," Daniel said, then added, "Some of our teammates are coming too. Chad's organizing it—says the team needs to show support."

"We'll probably go after I get home," Mariana said. "Maybe around five?"

Daniel nodded. "I'll text you if anything changes before then." He hesitated. "You holding up okay? People are talking a lot."

"I'm fine," Mariana said automatically.

Daniel clearly didn't believe her, but he didn't press. "Chad shut down some seniors who were saying stuff in the locker room. Told them Richey was a teammate and to show some respect."

The unexpected support from Chad—the team leader who had previously mocked Richey—touched Mariana. "Tell him thanks."

"Will do." Daniel glanced at the clock on the wall. "Better get to homeroom. Mrs. K will give us detention if we're late again."

As Daniel headed off, Jackie touched Mariana's arm gently. "See? People are on your side. On his side."

Mariana nodded, though she knew support from Daniel and Chad wouldn't shield her from the gossip machine that was already churning through the hallways. But it was something. A start.

They continued toward homeroom, the weight of stares and whispers following them like shadows. Just as they reached the door, Mariana's phone buzzed in her pocket. She pulled it out, her heart leaping when she saw the name: James Vance.

She stepped aside, motioning for Jackie to go ahead without her, and opened the message with trembling fingers.

James: Good news. They're starting to reduce sedation at 9. Doctor says response looks promising. Thought you'd want to know.

Relief flooded through her, so powerful she had to lean against the wall for support.

Mariana: Thank you for letting me know. Will come after school. Please keep me updated.

James: Will do. He's fighting.

Mariana slipped her phone back into her pocket, a small smile touching her lips despite the anxiety of the morning. Richey was fighting. Coming back. That knowledge gave her the strength to straighten up, to take a deep breath, and to step into the classroom with her head held high.

Mrs. Kowalowski was already at her desk, attendance sheet in hand. She looked up as Mariana entered, her expression softening momentarily before returning to its usual professional neutrality.

"Cutting it close, Mariana," she said, but without her usual sharpness.

"Sorry, Mrs. K."

As Mariana moved to her seat, she felt the weight of two dozen pairs of eyes following her progress. The room seemed to hold its collective breath—no one quite sure what to say, how to react to her presence after the weekend's drama.

She slid into her desk, the familiar feel of the smooth wood surface under her hands a small anchor in the surreal experience. Automatically, she glanced over her shoulder at the desk behind her—Richey's desk—and found it empty. Of course it was empty. He was in a hospital bed across town, machines breathing for him, doctors gradually reducing the medications that kept him unconscious.

But the sight of that vacant space hit her with unexpected force. The empty chair. The unoccupied desktop. The absence that everyone in the room was acutely aware of but no one mentioned.

Stephanie leaned over from the desk beside her. "You okay?" she whispered.

Mariana nodded, not trusting her voice.

"We heard he might be getting better," Stephanie continued, keeping her voice low. "Is that true?"

"They're starting to wake him up today," Mariana confirmed.

Stephanie's face lit up. "That's awesome! When will he be back?"

The question—so well-meaning, so naive—caught Mariana off guard. "I don't know," she admitted. "There's a lot of recovery ahead. Physical therapy. Maybe more surgeries."

"Oh." Stephanie's enthusiasm dimmed slightly. "But he will come back, right? Eventually?"

Before Mariana could answer, Mrs. Kowalowski called the class to order. "Alright, everyone. Eyes forward. Phones away. Just because it's Monday doesn't mean we're taking it easy."

As the class settled into its routine, Mariana found her gaze repeatedly drawn to the empty space behind her. She tried to imagine what it would be like when—if—Richey returned. Would he be the same person she'd connected with Friday night? Or would the accident have changed him in ways none of them could predict?

Dr. Mehta's cautious words echoed in her mind: *"The core of who he is should remain. But there may be changes. We need to be prepared for that possibility."*

Mariana forced her attention back to the front of the room, where Mrs. Kowalowski was reviewing the week's assignment schedule. One hour down. Six more to go. Then she could escape this fishbowl of stares and whispers, head to the hospital, and see for herself how Richey was progressing.

For now, she would face each class, each hallway transition, each curious or judgmental glance with the dignity her father had modeled for her. Head high. Eyes forward. The long view.

And if she occasionally glanced back at the empty desk, well, no one needed to know exactly what that space meant to her. Or how fervently she hoped to see it filled again.

First Breath

James Vance had never considered himself a religious man. The closest he came to prayer were the desperate bargains he'd made during hangovers, the half-sincere promises he'd offered to a God he wasn't sure was listening. But as he sat in Room 214, watching Dr. Mehta and a respiratory specialist prepare to remove Richey's ventilator, he found himself praying with the fervor of a true believer.

Please. Please. Please.

The words formed a silent litany in his mind, addressed to whatever higher power might be listening. The medical team moved with practiced efficiency, checking monitors, adjusting equipment, their voices hushed and professional.

"Mr. Vance," Dr. Mehta said, pausing beside him. "I want to prepare you for what's about to happen. We've been gradually reducing Richey's sedation since nine this morning. He's showing positive neurological responses—pain response in his extremities, some eye movement behind his lids. These are all good signs."

James nodded, his throat too tight for words.

"Once we remove the ventilator, he'll need to breathe on his own," she continued. "His last tests show his lung function has improved significantly, but there may be some initial struggle. This is normal. Try not to be alarmed."

"And if—" James swallowed hard. "If he can't breathe on his own?"

Dr. Mehta's expression remained calm but honest. "Then we'll reintubate immediately. But I believe he's ready."

The respiratory specialist, a stocky man with kind eyes and a thick mustache, approached the bed. "We're going to do this gradually," he explained. "First reducing the ventilator support, then removing the tube entirely. You may want to step out—"

"I'm staying," James interrupted firmly.

The specialist nodded, unsurprised. "Alright. Just try to remain calm for his sake. Even sedated, patients can sense anxiety in the room."

James took a deep breath, forcing his tense shoulders to relax. For Richey's sake, he would be a pillar of strength—or at least the appearance of it. He moved his chair slightly back from the bed, giving the medical team space to work, but kept his eyes fixed on his son's face.

Over the past three days, he had memorized every detail of Richey in this unnatural sleep—the exact rhythm of the ventilator's rise and fall, the particular tone of each monitor's beep, the way Richey's fingers sometimes twitched as if reaching for something just beyond his grasp. Now, all of that was about to change, and James wasn't sure if he was more terrified of things staying the same or of facing whatever came next.

"Beginning ventilator reduction," the respiratory specialist announced, adjusting settings on the machine.

Dr. Mehta stood on the opposite side of the bed, her attention divided between Richey's face and the monitors displaying his vital signs. A nurse positioned herself at the head of the bed, ready to assist.

James held his breath as the ventilator's rhythm changed, becoming less pronounced. The machine's mechanical hum shifted in tone and volume, each adjustment accompanied by a different pitched beep from the monitors. James's ears strained to distinguish between the routine sounds and potential warning signals. The room was warm from all the equipment, creating a stark contrast to the cool, sterile air that circulated from vents overhead. The sharp tang of alcohol swabs mingled with the unmistakable human scent of the medical team as they worked—clean sweat, mint breath, clinical soap. James's mouth went dry, the taste of hospital coffee bitter on his tongue as he watched each careful movement of the respiratory specialist's gloved hands.

Richey's chest continued to rise and fall, but the movement was different now—less mechanical, more tentative.

"Oxygen saturation at 94 percent," the nurse reported. "Heart rate increasing slightly."

"That's normal," Dr. Mehta assured James, noting his worried expression. "His body is responding to the change."

The respiratory specialist made another adjustment. "Reducing support to minimum settings."

James clenched his hands in his lap, fingernails digging into his palms. The minutes stretched like hours, each second marked by the steadily increasing beep of Richey's heart monitor.

"Oxygen holding at 93 percent," the nurse said. "Respiratory effort present."

Dr. Mehta nodded, satisfied. "He's initiating breaths on his own. Let's proceed with extubation."

The respiratory specialist glanced at James. "This part can be uncomfortable to watch. The tube removal sometimes triggers a gag reflex or coughing."

James steeled himself. "I understand."

They worked quickly then, the nurse suctioning Richey's mouth while the specialist deflated the small balloon that had held the tube in place. Then, with gentle but firm movements, he pulled the breathing tube from Richey's throat.

Richey's body immediately responded—a harsh cough, a grimace of discomfort, his head turning slightly to the side. James half-rose from his chair, instinct driving him toward his son, but Dr. Mehta held up a hand.

"Give him a moment," she said calmly. "Watch."

And James did watch, his own breathing suspended, as Richey's chest rose and fell—uneven at first, then settling into a rhythm. His own rhythm. No machine forcing air into his lungs. Just his body, remembering how to perform this most basic function of life.

"Oxygen saturation 91 percent and stabilizing," the nurse reported. "Heart rate returning to baseline."

"He's breathing," James whispered, the words barely audible.

Dr. Mehta smiled—a real smile, not the professional reassurance she usually offered. "Yes, he is. And quite well."

The respiratory specialist checked the monitors once more. "I'll place him on supplemental oxygen through a nasal cannula, just to support him while he adjusts. But he's doing the work himself now."

James watched as they positioned a thin tube beneath Richey's nostrils, securing it around his ears. Without the larger ventilator tube, Richey's face was more visible, more like himself. His lips were chapped, his skin pale, but he was breathing. On his own.

"What happens now?" James asked, his voice hoarse with emotion.

"We continue to monitor him closely," Dr. Mehta explained. "As the remaining sedation wears off, he may become more responsive. Don't expect immediate consciousness—it's more likely to be a gradual process. Moments of awareness interspersed with sleep."

"But he's coming back?" James needed to hear it confirmed, spelled out in clear terms.

"He's coming back," Dr. Mehta affirmed. "The next twenty-four hours will tell us more about his cognitive function, but this is a very positive step."

The medical team continued their work, checking connections, recording vitals, making adjustments to the various medications still flowing through Richey's IV. But James barely noticed them now. His focus had narrowed to the steady rise and fall of his son's chest—the miracle of that simple, automatic function he had taken for granted his entire life.

When they finally left, promising to return in thirty minutes for another check, James moved his chair closer to the bed. Now that the ventilator was gone, he could see more of Richey's face, could appreciate the subtle changes as his body navigated this new phase of healing.

"You did it, son," he said softly, taking Richey's hand. "You're breathing on your own now."

The monitors continued their steady rhythm. Richey's face remained still, but James imagined he could see a difference—some indefinable shift beneath the surface.

"The doctor says you might be able to hear me, even if you can't respond yet. So I want you to know I'm here. I haven't left." He paused, gathering himself. "And I'm so damn proud of you, Richey. So proud of how hard you're fighting."

Was it his imagination, or did Richey's fingers twitch slightly in his grasp? James watched, hardly daring to breathe, but there was no further movement. Still, the possibility lingered, feeding the hope that had been growing stronger with each positive report.

James glanced at his watch. Nearly four o'clock. Mariana would be out of school by now, possibly on her way. Daniel had visited during lunch, bringing a small cactus plant from his mother and a card signed by the football team. He'd watched in awe as the doctors explained the plan to remove the ventilator, his usual chattiness silenced by the gravity of the moment.

"You've got people pulling for you, Richey," James continued. "More than I realized. Your team came yesterday. Daniel's been checking in. And Mariana—" His voice softened. "She should be here soon. I think she'd be happy to see you breathing on your own."

He settled into the chair, maintaining his gentle hold on Richey's hand. Now that the immediate crisis of the ventilator removal had passed, the exhaustion of the past three days was catching up to him. He hadn't slept properly since Friday night—just brief naps in the hospital chair, his body never fully relaxing in case something changed while he wasn't watching.

But he couldn't sleep now. Not when Richey might wake at any moment, might need to see a familiar face when he first opened his eyes.

"I'm not going anywhere," James promised. "Whatever happens next, we face it together."

Mariana drove with both hands gripping the steering wheel, her attention focused on the road with an intensity that would have impressed her driving instructor. Her father's SUV felt enormous compared to the compact car she'd practiced on, and the responsibility of driving alone was still new enough to make her hyper-vigilant.

Her mother had been reluctant to let her drive to the hospital alone, but her father had intervened. "She has her license," he'd pointed out. "And it's a direct route. No highway driving." Unspoken was the understanding that this independence was a vote of confidence—a recognition of Mariana's maturity in handling the events of the past few days.

The school day had been as difficult as she'd expected. Classes had proceeded with their usual rhythm, but nothing about them had felt normal. Every teacher had treated her with careful consideration, either avoiding any mention of the accident or expressing awkward sympathy. Her classmates had oscillated between strained normalcy and obvious curiosity, the whispers following her through hallways and cafeteria alike.

But none of that mattered now. James's text after last period had changed everything: *Ventilator removed successfully. Breathing on his own.*

Eight simple words that had made her knees weak with relief, had given her the courage to ask for the car keys, had propelled her through Houston traffic with a mixture of anxiety and desperate hope.

As she pulled into the hospital parking lot, she spotted a familiar figure—Eleanor Vance, Richey's mother, must have arrived from the East Coast. The woman was climbing out of a taxi, suitcase beside her, her posture tight with worry. Mariana recognized her from the photograph in Richey's room—older now, her light brown hair streaked with silver, but with the same elegant features that Richey had inherited.

Mariana parked carefully, then sat for a moment, watching as Eleanor disappeared through the hospital's main entrance. What would it be like, she wondered, to return after years away and find your son in such a state? To face your ex-husband across a hospital bed instead of a courtroom?

She pushed the thoughts aside and gathered her backpack. Those weren't her questions to answer. Her role here was simpler—to support Richey, to check on his progress, to be a friend. Whatever complicated family dynamics played out in Room 214 were for the Vances to navigate.

As she approached the hospital entrance, her phone buzzed with a text from Daniel: *Saw him earlier. Looking better without the tube. Let me know how he is now.*

She smiled slightly, appreciating Daniel's steady presence through all of this. He had been a constant at school today, appearing between classes to check on her, deflecting questions from other students, creating a buffer of normalcy in the swirl of gossip.

Just arriving, she replied. *Will update you later.*

The hospital's familiar environment enveloped her as she made her way to the elevators—the antiseptic smell, the squeak of rubber-soled shoes on tile, the hushed voices and muted beeping from various rooms. She had been here only two days, yet already the route to Room 214 was embedded in her memory.

As the elevator doors opened on the ICU floor, Mariana steeled herself for whatever she might find. James's text had been positive, but the reality of seeing Richey without the ventilator—more present, more himself, but perhaps still trapped in unconsciousness—filled her with nervous anticipation.

The nurse at the station looked up as Mariana approached, recognition softening her expression. "You're back," she said. "He's having a good day."

"I heard they removed the ventilator," Mariana said.

The nurse nodded. "About an hour ago. He's doing well with it. And his mother arrived from out of town." She glanced toward Room 214. "They might appreciate a little space for the family reunion."

Mariana hesitated. "Should I come back tomorrow? I don't want to intrude."

The nurse considered this, then shook her head. "No, I think a quick visit would be fine. Mr. Vance has mentioned you several times. Just keep it brief, alright?"

"Of course. Thank you."

Mariana approached Room 214 cautiously, unsure of the etiquette for interrupting a family moment. The door was partially open, voices filtering into the hallway. She knocked gently.

The door swung open, revealing James Vance. His face lit up when he saw her. "Mariana," he said warmly. "Come in, please."

She stepped inside, immediately aware of the woman standing on the other side of Richey's bed. Eleanor Vance looked up, her eyes—the same shade of blue as Richey's—assessing Mariana with surprised interest.

"Eleanor," James said, "this is Mariana Garcia. She's, uh—"

"A friend of Richey's," Mariana supplied quickly, extending her hand across the bed. "It's nice to meet you, Mrs. Vance. I'm so sorry it's under these circumstances."

Eleanor took her hand, her grip firm despite her apparent exhaustion. "Thank you for coming," she said, her voice carrying the faint traces of a Southern accent. "James has mentioned how supportive you've been."

Mariana's gaze shifted to Richey, and she felt a surge of emotion at the sight of him without the ventilator tube. A thin oxygen line ran beneath his nose, but his face was more visible now, more his own. His chest rose and fell with natural rhythm, a simple miracle that brought tears to her eyes.

"He's breathing," she whispered.

James nodded, pride evident in his expression. "Has been for over an hour now. Doctors are very pleased with his oxygen levels."

"Has he shown any signs of waking up?" Mariana asked, unable to tear her eyes from Richey's face.

"Not yet," Eleanor replied, adjusting the blanket over Richey's chest with maternal care. "But they say that's normal. The remaining sedation needs time to clear his system."

An awkward silence fell over the room, the three of them connected only by their concern for the unconscious boy in the bed. Mariana felt suddenly intrusive, an outsider in this family tableau.

"I should probably go," she said. "Give you both some privacy."

"No, please," Eleanor said, surprising Mariana with her insistence. "I was just about to find some coffee. It's been a long day of travel." She glanced at James. "Perhaps you could show me where the cafeteria is?"

James looked between Eleanor and Mariana, understanding dawning in his eyes. "Of course," he said. "We'll give you a few minutes, Mariana. Can I bring you anything?"

"No, thank you. I'm fine."

Eleanor gathered her purse, then paused beside Mariana. "James tells me you were with Richey before the accident," she said quietly. "That you've been here every day since."

Mariana nodded, uncertain what else to say.

"Thank you," Eleanor said simply. "For caring about my son."

After they left, Mariana stood for a moment, slightly overwhelmed by the unexpected kindness from Richey's mother. Then she moved to take the chair James had vacated, sliding it close to the bed.

Up close, she could see the improvements in Richey's condition more clearly. The swelling had continued to decrease, the bruising fading to yellowish-green around the edges. His lips were chapped but pink, no longer compressed around the breathing tube. She could almost imagine he was simply sleeping.

"Hey," she said softly, taking his hand. "It's Mariana. I came as soon as school let out."

No response, but she hadn't really expected one. Still, she took comfort in the warmth of his hand, in the steady beep of his heart monitor.

"School was weird today," she continued, settling into the one-sided conversation that had become their routine. "Everyone's talking, but I just ignored it. Your desk was empty in first period. Mrs. K didn't say anything, but I could tell she noticed."

She stroked the back of his hand with her thumb, careful to avoid the IV line. "Daniel's been great. He visited earlier, right? Brought you a cactus from his mom. Says it's hard to kill, even for guys like you two."

Mariana smiled faintly, remembering Daniel's awkward attempt at humor. "The football team is behind you too. Chad, of all people, has been shutting down rumors in the locker room. Coach Kenneck held a special team meeting this morning."

She paused, gathering her thoughts. "I, um, talked to Jackie today. She apologized. Feels terrible about what happened. I'm not sure I'm ready to forgive her completely, but... I understand it wasn't entirely her fault."

The steady rhythm of the monitors filled the silence between her words. Outside the room, hospital life continued—nurses' voices, the squeak of carts, the distant chime of an elevator. But inside, time seemed suspended, measured only in Richey's breaths and heartbeats.

"Your mom seems nice," Mariana continued. "She came all the way from the East Coast. And your dad—" She smiled. "He's been amazing, Richey. Hasn't left your side. Hasn't been drinking. He's really trying."

She leaned closer, her voice dropping to a near whisper. "I need you to wake up soon. There's so much I want to tell you. So much I want to know about you." Her voice caught. "Friday night wasn't enough. It was just the beginning."

Richey remained still, his face peaceful in unconsciousness. But Mariana continued, the words coming more easily now that she'd started.

As she spoke, her mind drifted to another beginning, another moment when everything had shifted. She was fourteen, a freshman at Memorial High, standing nervously at the natatorium doors before her first major high school competition.

Her stomach had been in knots, her new team swimsuit feeling too tight, too professional. Too much like a promise she wasn't sure she could keep. The older girls on the team barely knew her name—she was just the freshman with the good times in practice, the one Coach Riley had pulled up to varsity unusually early.

"You don't belong here," she'd whispered to herself, staring at her reflection in the glass doors, seeing only a scared immigrant girl playing dress-up in a champion's suit.

"First meet?"

She'd turned to find an upperclassman watching her—a senior, Emma Rodriguez, the team captain and Central Texas record holder in the 200 butterfly.

Mariana had nodded, not trusting her voice.

"I threw up before my first high school meet," Emma had said matter-of-factly. "Right in the pool. They had to delay the start by thirty minutes."

Despite her nerves, Mariana had laughed, surprised by the confession.

Emma had smiled. "The secret isn't not being scared. It's using the fear. When you dive in, all that nervous energy becomes power." She'd adjusted Mariana's cap with practiced hands. "You've got something special, Garcia. We all see it. Now go show everyone else."

Mariana had swum like she was possessed that day, setting a freshman record and earning her place on the team not through her potential but through her performance. Emma's words had changed something fundamental in how she saw herself—not as an imposter, but as someone who belonged.

Now, sitting beside Richey's hospital bed, Mariana realized that was exactly what he'd given her at the party—that same sense of belonging, of being seen without judgment. In all the noise and chaos of teenage social hierarchies, their conversation had been like coming up for air after too long underwater.

"You've got something special too, Richey," she whispered, squeezing his hand gently. "I saw it right away. And I'm still here, waiting for you to show everyone else."

"I know we barely know each other. I know it probably sounds crazy. But when we talked that night—when you really listened to me, when you told me about your dad, when we sat outside under the stars—it felt like I'd known you forever." She blinked back tears. "Like I was finally meeting someone who saw me. The real me."

She squeezed his hand gently. "So you have to wake up, okay? You have to come back. Because I think... I think this could be something important. Something real."

The monitors beeped steadily, unchanged by her confession. Mariana sighed, feeling slightly foolish for pouring out her heart to someone who couldn't respond. But then—

A slight pressure against her palm. So faint she might have imagined it.

She froze, staring at their joined hands. "Richey?"

There it was again—the slightest tightening of his fingers around hers. Not a random muscle spasm, but a deliberate squeeze. Weak, barely perceptible, but unmistakably intentional.

Mariana's heart leaped into her throat. "Richey? Can you hear me?"

No further response came. His face remained still, his eyes closed. But that brief pressure—that momentary connection—was enough to send hope surging through her veins like lightning.

He had heard her. Somewhere in the depths of sedation and injury, he had registered her presence, her voice, her words. And he had reached back, bridging the gap between consciousness and whatever twilight state he occupied.

Mariana pressed the call button with her free hand, her eyes never leaving Richey's face, her other hand maintaining its gentle hold on his. "He squeezed my hand," she told the nurse who answered. "Just now. Twice."

"I'll let Dr. Mehta know," the nurse said, her professional tone not quite masking her excitement. "This is a very good sign."

As the nurse hurried away, Mariana continued to watch Richey, waiting for any further indication of awareness. None came—no additional squeeze, no flutter of eyelids, no change in breathing pattern. But it didn't matter. That single moment of connection was enough to sustain her, to fuel the hope that had been growing since James's text.

"I'm here," she whispered, leaning close enough that her words brushed his ear. "And I'm not going anywhere."

Outside the room, footsteps approached—James and Eleanor returning, probably alerted by the nurse. In a moment, the quiet intimacy would give way to medical assessments and parental concern. But for now, in this brief interval between heartbeats, it was just the two of them—connected by the gentle pressure of fingers against palm, by words spoken and heard, by the first tentative bridge spanning the distance between unconsciousness and awakening.

Mariana smiled through her tears, still holding Richey's hand as if it were the most precious thing in the world. "Welcome back," she whispered.

About the Author

Rodolfo E. Köng was born in Guatemala City and immigrated to the U.S. at age 11. He holds degrees in Engineering and Theology and works as a consultant across industries. A longtime mentor in faith and youth formation, he writes stories that explore identity, sacrifice, and resilience. His work is shaped by a belief in purpose, perseverance, and the quiet power of human connection.